THE
MIRACLE

KAMAL DHILLON

BALBOA.PRESS
A DIVISION OF HAY HOUSE

Copyright © 2020 Kamal Dhillon.

All rights reserved. No part of this book may be used or reproduced by any means, graphic, electronic, or mechanical, including photocopying, recording, taping or by any information storage retrieval system without the written permission of the author except in the case of brief quotations embodied in critical articles and reviews.

Balboa Press books may be ordered through booksellers or by contacting:

Balboa Press
A Division of Hay House
1663 Liberty Drive
Bloomington, IN 47403
www.balboapress.com
844-682-1282

Because of the dynamic nature of the Internet, any web addresses or links contained in this book may have changed since publication and may no longer be valid. The views expressed in this work are solely those of the author and do not necessarily reflect the views of the publisher, and the publisher hereby disclaims any responsibility for them.

The author of this book does not dispense medical advice or prescribe the use of any technique as a form of treatment for physical, emotional, or medical problems without the advice of a physician, either directly or indirectly. The intent of the author is only to offer information of a general nature to help you in your quest for emotional and spiritual well-being. In the event you use any of the information in this book for yourself, which is your constitutional right, the author and the publisher assume no responsibility for your actions.

Any people depicted in stock imagery provided by Getty Images are models, and such images are being used for illustrative purposes only. Certain stock imagery © Getty Images.

Print information available on the last page.

ISBN: 978-1-9822-5604-3 (sc)
ISBN: 978-1-9822-5602-9 (hc)
ISBN: 978-1-9822-5603-6 (e)

Library of Congress Control Number: 2020919109

Balboa Press rev. date: 10/02/2020

Dedicated to

All those who have kept their beautiful dreams alive

Gratitude to

My Mom and Dad for lifetime love and support – You make me strong

Special Thanks to

Rajbir Sandhu, editor (and my husband) for making this dream come true

Big Thank You

To the reader for giving your precious time

We are all

in a

caravan

each one

of our own

The Journey of this Story

That morning I missed the dawn, the sunrise. I sat in the balcony with my cup of coffee, a little disenchanted. Coffee felt bitter too. A big white seagull flapped its wings and flew over the nearby pond. Two goslings attempted little jumps and skidded over the thin icy sheet of snow. A couple of geese beaked together in the morning romance. Even without the sun, the morning had come to life. I noticed the tranquility of the steel-grey sky. Some white patches of clouds came floating by. Now the sky looked like an old woman with her flowing white hair, looking down and admiring the movements of life.

This was the beginning of the book. Sitting there, I realized how we start getting used to specific ways of life. We get used to a certain way of living, sipping coffee in the same mug, conversing the same way with certain people, or working in the same job day in and day out. We get used to keeping our pillows snuggled in a certain way or sit in a certain posture. We get accustomed to smiling halfway and to people's reactions in a particular way. We get used to life happening precisely the way it happens each day, every day.

Before we realize, we have closed ourselves in an invisible mental box of certainties. We stop knowing more, exploring more. All that is left is an accumulation – of opinions, judgments, ideas, possessions ... Before long, the box becomes full – no more fresh air and no room for growth. We forget who we were, what we wanted, where we lost ourselves till something significant jolts us. Our glass castle falls apart, and the shards pierce our daily life. Then we begin to despair, become restless, heartbroken. It hurts at that time like nothing else before.

And then one fine day, yes, one fine day, it all changes! The universe opens the box. A fresh breeze comes in, blowing away all that is unwanted and stale. Space is created for knowing. We drop everything and surrender. The universe extends its arms of immense love, embraces us, caresses us, and brings us home – to ourselves! Out heart beats again – thump, thump, thump.

Enjoy – The Miracle.

Kamal Dhillon

The Author's Journey

We all have a story to tell, and each story has its phases, its chapters. I feel that even after years of living, I am a mystery even to myself, still discovering life. This is a synopsis of my life … my life so far! Before I reached here, a flashback will probably describe my journey from there to here.

An event in my twenties changed everything for me, and my life became a complete nightmare … from a carefree butterfly, I turned into a fearful soul and lost my self-esteem. So much so that even a little loud sound would make me cry. I felt crushed. Even after a few years of getting out of that situation, I continued to live in fear. There was a lot of pain in the heart. I lost my belief in any goodness. My melancholic poetry flowed ceaselessly. I wrote pages after pages and filled diaries, which I threw in the garbage, out of pain and frustration. All of that grief-stricken, wistful, and despairing writing would set a mood for nothing but self-pity.

But then something shifted inside me. It seemed as if the universe was all out to reimburse for those strayed moments of my happiness. Platonic relationships from far and wide started pooling in, and I became a part of the universal clan. The perennial trickling of love now burst open the floodgates, soaking the unadulterated heart in a colorful essence of life. Fulfillment is an inner story; perhaps we need to learn between the lines ...

Experiences grew, life became a prayer, and a selfless living became my identity. My trust in life bloomed. The lively, upbeat 'me' returned, this time with gratitude for a second chance to revive. Often, I danced and danced ... listened to uplifting music. The universe reciprocated abundantly and filled my heart with joy. Life since then has been a never-ending blessing, with acceptance of all its ups and downs. It still is! I no more question things that did not work out, that pained me, haunted me and did not let me meet my-self for years and years.

Now I am able to connect to all beautiful souls who the universe chooses and brings in my life. I know not where my path is leading me. I am flowing the Tao way ... just surrender ... and let life row the boat. Flow is acceptance, allowance, flow is *as is*!

I am so blessed that you, the precious people, are brought in my life. This is not your or my plan to connect ... it is that Pure Energy which always brings the best for us and knows the right way – in all ways!

Love again, live again, give yourself another chance, and another. Start fresh every time. Close your eyes and listen to the divine orchestra. Join in the dance of bliss, clap with this marvelous show. Drop everything today and allow yourself to become one with That – What Is!

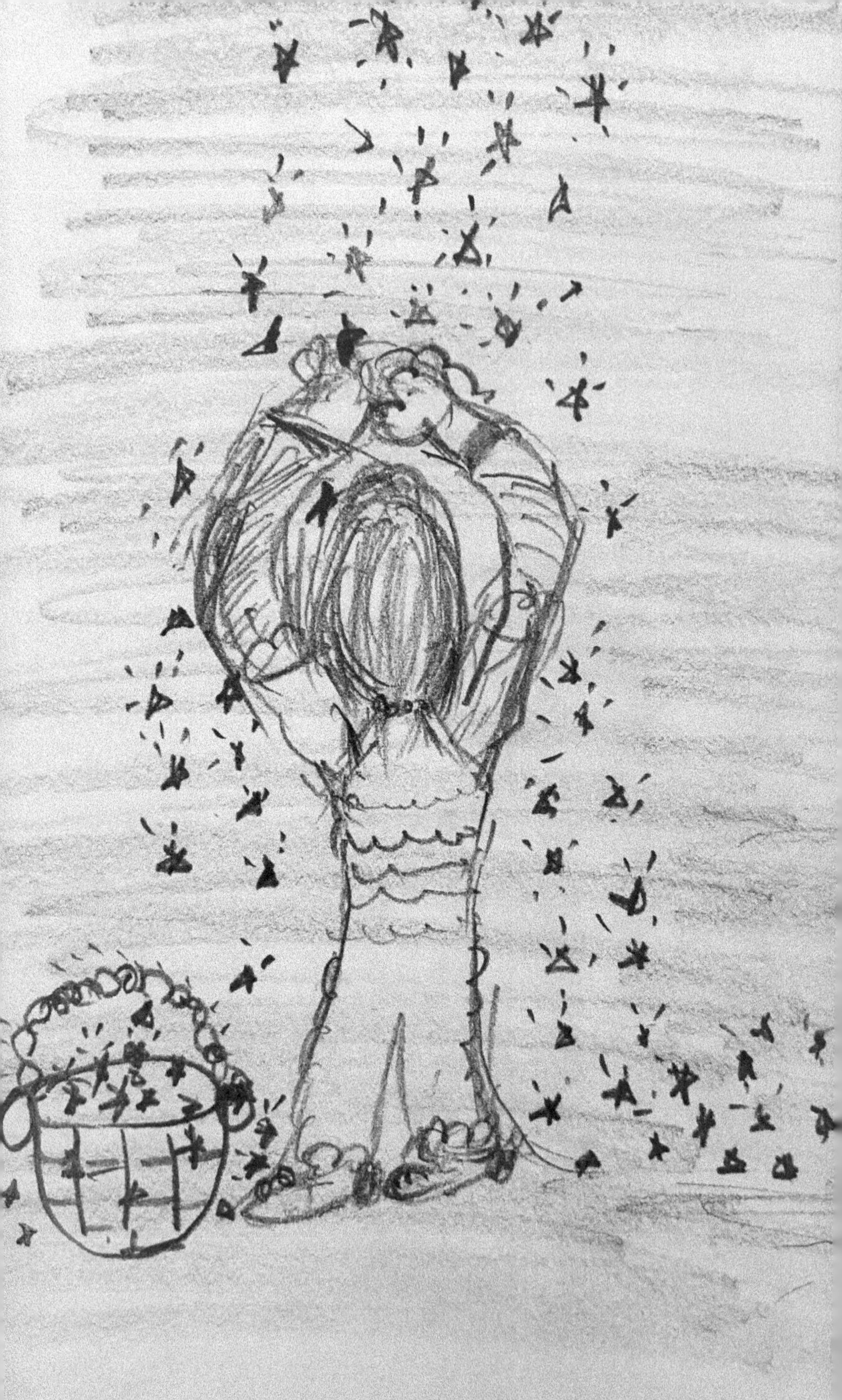

My Gratitude

I am grateful to the universe that I have finally learned to *accept what is* and *allow* all that is coming my way, *without judgment*.

I am grateful to the universe for letting me learn *acceptance of all existence, as is*.

I am grateful to the universe, for it brought me to this point where I am able to *let go of memories of experiences that are no longer needed, without resentment*.

I am grateful that I am able to *forgive those I believed were wrongdoers in my view*, and that way, *I forgive my inner-self and free my soul of any burden*.

I am grateful to the universe for making me understand that *I am a valued and essential participant in the play of life, and so is everyone else.*

I am grateful to be given the wisdom that *even when happenings are not to my liking, that is how they are supposed to be.*

I am grateful to the universe for making me a happy survivor. *Better, not bitter.*

I have understood that I am a *work in progress, flawed, far from perfect,* and that's how it is meant to be.

I am traveling light and happy, finally ...

In gratitude

Kamal

I am surprised
even after
decades
of my life together
with you
O world –
you haven't
met me

Contents

The Dream 1

The Beginning 7

The Meeting 11

The Knowing 30

The Connection 38

The Mantra 45

The Healing 53

The Love 57

The Sharing 67

The Pilgrimage 82

The Introspection 91

The Ease 101

The Contemplation 108

The Enlightenment 115

The Epiphany 136

The Miracle 143

The Dream

That morning felt noticeably distinct. A deep orange hue of the rising sun had spread its giant wings, enveloping the entire sky. The color canopy created by nature in the backdrop was enchanting and soothing. With some merging ash grey clouds, it felt as if a sage, garbed in a large orange robe, had woken up after a long season of meditation and was ready to walk down the abundant mountains of the Himalayas. Yes, it was a different morning, perhaps forecasting a significant change somewhere.

Under this vast expanse of colorful sheets of the sky sat a man, motionless, on the precipice of a big rugged rock. The strong wind of the afternoon heat did not seem to match with the storm of questions in his head. His long peppery beard vigorously shook with the gusts of the wind, and his unkempt hair collected more dust than ever before. "Where do I belong? The people I was born to or the people I grew up with? Those who stayed with me or those who disappeared in the haze of life? The streets and cities I traveled or the places I visit in my dreams? The work of everyday life or the solitary self inside me? Am I a part of the group, or am I by myself? Do I belong to the One up there, or am I whole of the universe? Where, where, where do I belong?" This rattle of questions was not there before, at least not before that day. In one moment, this man felt the wisdom of a saint flowing through him, and in the very next moment, he questioned his existence. "Nothing to be, nowhere to go, all is as is … follow this Amoor … All is as is … All is as is …" echoed a voice around his ears continuously, and the sound grew louder and louder. "All is as is … follow your heart … come home … wake up, Amoor … wake up …"

"Ohhh … ohhh … ohhh!" Amoor sat up in his bed, his hands covering his ears, gasping for breath. Beads of sweat trickled down from his forehead to his eyebrows.

"Ahhh … this dream felt so real and absurd," he whispered in disbelief at the contents of the dream.

"Was that me in the dream?" He tried to decode the dream.

"Kuhooo … kuhoooo … kuhooooo …" Amoor's thought stream was interrupted before he could go any further by the alarm clock that had started singing a tune of songbirds and lapping waters of a river. He got down from his bed slowly, still little dazed, and opened the curtains of the bedroom. To his surprise, the sky looked the same as the one he had seen in the dream – deep orange.

"This is so strange!" Amoor murmured to himself, his mind going back to the dream. But then, he brushed off all thoughts as he thought of Alie, his wife, who had gone on a vacation with their two children. Perhaps a part of his heart missed her. "She always sleeps like a baby," looking at her bedside, he thought. He couldn't remember the last time he had slept soundly. Alie had tried to convince him to join them in the vacation, but he couldn't take a break from his ever-busy work life.

"Krrr … krrrr … krrrrr …" The loud buzzer of another alarm clock startled Amoor. He had never liked the sound of this old-style clock. But it was a good idea to have a second alarm clock buzzing, just in case the first one didn't wake him up.

Amoor liked to follow a set routine, and, like him, his grip on it was tenacious. He preferred to live a very regimented and pre-carved life. He wore the same style of business suits to work. He ate his breakfast with great dedication at a fixed time. His route to his office was always the same – same highway, same stops, almost the exact timings. In fact, he cloned his life each day.

On that fateful day, the day of the dream, Amoor turned on the news channel before heading to the office, as per his morning routine. To his mental pique, the traffic update mentioned that the highway he routinely traveled on was shut down due to a major accident. Amoor's head and stomach tightened immediately. He always resisted unusual alterations in his daily routine.

"Ah, I hate this!" he frowned at the thought of another different beginning of the day. "That dream, and now this."

Amoor took a heavy breath. Shaking his head in disagreement with the little changes in the morning, he headed to his washroom to get ready for his office. Soon he was all set to go. He walked down the peacock-blue carpeted stairs from his second-floor master bedroom. Quickly, he walked past his grand living room. Over the years, Amoor had amassed a significant fortune and bought whatever he took a fancy to. The living room was tastefully decorated with the most beautiful collectibles from all over the world. Still, over time he had forgotten to pause and look at those treasures that he had once felt so passionate about. These possessions were now nothing more than a collage of displays. Lately, despite having acquired everything that he wanted, a feeling of emptiness … a kind of void lingered in Amoor's heart.

As the clock struck nine, he stepped out of his house, clutching his leather briefcase, thinking of an alternate route to the office. From immaculately styled hair to the sharp tips of his shiny shoes, Amoor was a statement of luxury, pride, and discipline. All this opulence, however, had come at a steep price and could barely compensate for the lost peace of mind. Work, work, and more work – that had become the mantra of his life.

Weather changes
every now and then
warm air
gets heated
and scorches the face...
cool breeze
benumbs the body
bursts of rain
drown the newly born hopes
and ancient dreams
unfulfilled...
will it ever change?
Mind takes a sprint
along the relation route
and crawls
back, tired
people jogging
along with life
for years and years
waiting to be
fit sometimes,
like a soft rock
age withers away
And I sigh...
witnessing all that
turning into dust
I am
maybe
an observer

The Beginning

Amoor opened the door of his red car that he had recently bought and plummeted into the driver's seat. Driving his own car – this was the second change in his routine in a single day – his chauffeur had called in sick.

"What a day! It sucks!" Amoor grumbled. The corners of his mouth curved down automatically to sync with the unhappiness of his mind.

He started the car, and instantly the GPS swung up in front of the dashboard. Amoor entered the destination address, "All set to go! Drive safely!" the automated female voice started giving instructions on the new route. His head felt more relaxed with the expectation of regaining control of the day.

Amoor pressed the accelerator, and within seconds the car engine revved up. Soon he was on the highway, weaving in and out of traffic in the blink of an eye. He had not driven this car much; mostly, his chauffeur drove it. But he had not lost his touch. As his car picked up speed, so did his thoughts.

"Now everything will happen as planned. At 11:00, the investors will sit for the meeting, and I will settle finances for forever." Amoor's ever-active mind had already started etching out the plan of the day of his well-planned life.

Lost in the intricate net of his thoughts, he did not realize that he had taken a wrong exit on the highway.

"Wrong exit … too late!" a voice sprang from Amoor's head.

"What the hell!" Amoor's jaw tightened. Veins in his temples started bulging as he grimaced, beating himself up for this lapse in attention. He was already frustrated with the happenings of the day. Now this wrong exit threw him out of gear completely.

In reality, *it was not a wrong exit; it was a different exit*. Amoor had no idea that this one single different exit will be an entrance to an entirely new life experience. Ruffled, Amoor got engrossed in the multiple voices in his head, all vying for immediate attention. He did not realize that the road ahead was wet from the rains of the previous night. While all the mental conversation was in full bloom, the car careened with a sudden buzzing noise. Amoor's heart started pounding. His stomach turned into a knot. Shocked at this another unusual happening, he tried to steer the car to safety but lost control. The vehicle veered off the curb of the slick road and skidded down the steep slope, tumbling down with sparks flying off the red rims of the tires.

Boom … boom … bang!

The car came to an abrupt halt with a big jolt. Amoor's body shook completely. His throat dried up, and his lips became parched, his perfectly gelled hair in a mess as he hit his head on the side of the window. The air inside the car became suffocating. He could hardly breathe. There was total darkness for a few seconds, and his sight became blurred. His eyes started closing despite his best effort to be awake. The last thing he saw was grey smoke billowing from the front of the car. Amoor became unconscious.

In moments of solitude
throwing back
my tired arms
my talking mind
my restless body,
I let everything
be still
silent
mute,
no sound of the wind
no calls of the wild
simply
in my
own being...
sometimes
my self needs
to be
myself

The Meeting

"Ahhh …" Amoor opened his eyes after a while, sighing with pain.

"Where am I?" he moaned, quite perplexed.

He touched his forehead, felt a bump, and rubbed it to comfort himself. "Ohhh …" He felt the pain again.

Using all his strength and with tremendous effort, he pushed open the door of the car and got out. What he saw was shocking. The front of his car had turned into mangled metal. The windshield had smashed into pieces. As if in oblivion, Amoor touched his body to see if he was okay. His eyes closed momentarily; no bones were broken, just bruises. He was alive. It was a miracle!

Suddenly, Amoor felt a little sting on his wrist. The glass of his expensive watch had shattered into pieces. He pulled the watch off his wrist and threw it towards the seat of the car. He was still not able to fully comprehend that he had met with such a severe accident. Amoor staggered. Trying to regain his balance, he put his hands on the car's roof. A feeling of sadness shrouded him at that moment. He blamed himself for not being focused while driving. *Guilt is the home of sorrow.*

"How can this happen to me? I'm always so careful. How did I lose control?" A series of thoughts started reproaching him. "And no one came to help! That's bizarre! Why is it so quiet here?" Once again, a multitude of questions ran through his bewildered mind.

Regaining some composure, Amoor looked around. He realized that he was somewhere amidst a kind of a jungle. The velvety green moss on the barks of the trees and the smell of wet woods lent a mystical aura to the place. Around were many lush canopies of red and yellow gulmohar trees where bees hummed and circled, going in and out of giant honeycombs that hung vertically. Rows of drooping banana trees were laden with purple flowers, and scores of ripe banana bunches dotted the landscape.

An abundance of guava, papaya, and mango trees added to the lushness of the place. The crisp, elliptical, green leaves of large banyan and peepal trees rustled with the gentle breeze. A few grey squirrels and white rabbits hopped over the knotted stems and disappeared in the hollows of these trees. Although the scene was stunningly mesmerizing, there was no human presence.

Amoor felt a little scared.

He collected himself and after a few seconds, almost screamed, "Heyyyy … anyone around?"

There was no response. Amoor's voice echoed and got lost in the wilderness.

Panic-stricken, he shouted again, "Hello … hello … anyone there? I need help!"

He heard nothing back in response.

"Hel…l…o…o…o…" This time he almost choked.

He heard the crackling of dead branches on the ground as if someone was walking over them.

"Who … who is there?" Amoor yelled assertively, trying to simulate some courage.

"Hello!" Suddenly, a soft, soothing voice greeted him.

Amoor looked around, trying to figure out the source of the voice. There was no one in sight.

"I am here!" The voice came again from close by.

Amoor looked in the direction of the voice. A little boy was peeping his head out from behind a mango tree. Amoor's heart felt comforted seeing another person. He had never felt that much preciousness of the presence of a human being. Never. It felt so typical always to have other people around him, but without that feeling of interconnectedness.

"Hey, come here," said Amoor in a husky, authoritarian voice — a voice that had controlled the businesses of the large multinational company he headed.

The boy smiled and came closer. He had a shaven head except for a tiny braid in the center. He was wearing a pastel yellow robe-like loose shirt and a matching bell-bottomed pajama, slightly rising above the heels. A long rosary of emerald stones swung around his neck carelessly. Amoor noticed his beautiful, deep expressive eyes and intensely calm face. The boy had a very charismatic appearance.

"He must be ten or eleven, looks so different from boys of his age," thought Amoor, looking at the boy carefully.

"Come here! I need some help! Do you live here? What is this place? Is there anyone who can get me home?" Amoor's questions came in a torrent.

The boy looked at him curiously, took two steps ahead. He touched Amoor's hand in a patting motion and replied in a very comforting tone, "You are safe and well, and that is all that matters at this moment."

"What?" mumbled Amoor as his ever-talking head suddenly became silent after hearing this unusual reply from a boy of such tender age. He wanted to say something more but couldn't.

"Come with me, and I'll take you home." The boy's voice was reassuring.

He held Amoor's right hand, and they started taking the first few steps of their journey together. Amoor so much wanted to resist that direction, that feeling of being guided, that disarming voice, but something held him magically. He quietly started to follow the little boy, speechless and numb, as if he were in a dream.

Amoor had always lived a life that controlled and led other people. His word was 'The Command' for those in his office and at home. He had been a leader, a decision-maker, a direction giver. And here, for the first time in his life, a little boy had taken charge of him with nothing but a sweet, irresistible voice and a smile.

"Who are you?" Amoor questioned, as he found the silence a bit uncomfortable.

"Me? I am nothing, just a child of the universe. People call me Little Sensei," replied the boy, slightly turning his head towards Amoor.

"Hmm." Amoor could only say this much. The unexpected response from the boy took him by surprise, but he chose not to pay much attention. His throat had become dry due to thirst.

The little boy sensed the dryness in Amoor's voice and quickly pulled out a small bottle of water.

"Here, have some water!"

Amoor grabbed the bottle and gulped it down his throat.

"Thank you!" said Amoor, gratefully, impressed by the acute perception of the young boy.

The boy stopped after walking a few steps and scratched his head as if thinking and said, "Mmm … let me get you a couple of bananas. You must be hungry." Then, without waiting for Amoor's reply, he reached for the drooping leaves of a banana tree, pulled down the branch, and plucked two ripe bananas.

"Here, have these," he gave both the bananas to Amoor and resumed walking.

"Wow, you are fast as lightning!" said Amoor, taking the bananas. "Won't you eat?" The hard shell of Amoor had become a little porous.

"Nah, I ate roti some time back. But, thanks anyway," replied the boy and continued walking.

Amoor was very hungry. He quickly peeled one banana after the other, took big bites, and caught up with Sensei. He was beginning to take a liking to this enigmatic little boy.

Walking behind Sensei, the mysterious silence of the place held Amoor in its embrace; the tension in his body and mind started easing slightly. This place was so much quieter than the one he had been living in with its constant noise, honking of car horns, and sirens of fire trucks. It was so peaceful here that he could hear the chirping of the birds and croaking of the frogs in this rainy season. He could even hear his heartbeats. Now and then, fresh drops of rainwater resting on the branches and leaves dropped on his gaunt face. A bubbling creek flowed without any resistance along its path, jumping past small stones.

"I love the flow of things, Sir. See how everything around here is in tune with the rhythm of the day," said Sensei smiling, corresponding to Amoor's thoughts.

"My name is Amoor Reasat," interrupted Amoor quickly.

"I think 'Amoor' is easy to remember," said Sensei, "We'll soon discover the rest of you."

"What! Discover me? That sounds quite strange!" blurted Amoor off the cuff, his face flushing.

"Yes, we will soon discover you, Amoor!" Sensei ventured. "We all have a name given to us after birth, which is an acceptable social norm. But we spend all our life identifying with the name or the form or living up to its image. Isn't it so? We are blends of environment, conditioning, and circumstances. In most part, we don't even meet our real selves. Have you ever noticed that *we live what we learn and not live who we are?*"

"Huh?"

Amoor was taken aback with this unanticipated, intense mini-sermon. His lips got sealed, but, as always, his mind was an active articulator – a running commentary commenced in his head.

"Who the heck is this boy! How did he just say something so profound? And why am I listening to him? Why am I even here? It is all so uncanny!" Amoor was somewhat perplexed, even a little annoyed. Sensei had said something exceptional for his age.

It seemed that the journey of these two strangers, walking along the creek, under the dense trees, and on the muddy path, was to be filled with tremendous thought-provoking instances.

Soon, the rugged path started merging into a smooth pathway, perhaps carved by the footsteps of many passers-by. At a distance, the ripe mustard fields were spread in golden sheets, adding a lustrous yellow color to the already bright day. Even though the walk was quite scenic, Amoor was not very comfortable walking – his shoes were hurting him.

"Isn't it beautiful, Amoor?" Sensei's question broke the chain of spiraling thoughts in Amoor's mind.

Amoor simply nodded as he looked around. He realized that in the commotion of city life, his version of beauty had become limited to the tall and gleaming skyscrapers and human-made manicured parks with little varieties of small trees and shrubs. Nature was either hushed away from the cities or lingered in remnants on the terraces and in the balcony flowerpots.

"This is absolutely enchanting," whispered Amoor as he looked around and took in a lungful of fresh air, after a long time. "But wait," suddenly Amoor stopped for a moment, looked at his shoes, and took them off. His feet finally felt free.

"Would you be fine to walk without shoes, Amoor?" Sensei looked back and inquired.

"I don't know, maybe." There was some hesitation in Amoor's voice.

"Ok," Sensei shrugged his shoulders and gave a little tug to his braid.

Amoor felt the cool soil like a balm for his aching feet. He walked carefully so as not to get hurt by the dry twigs lying on the path.

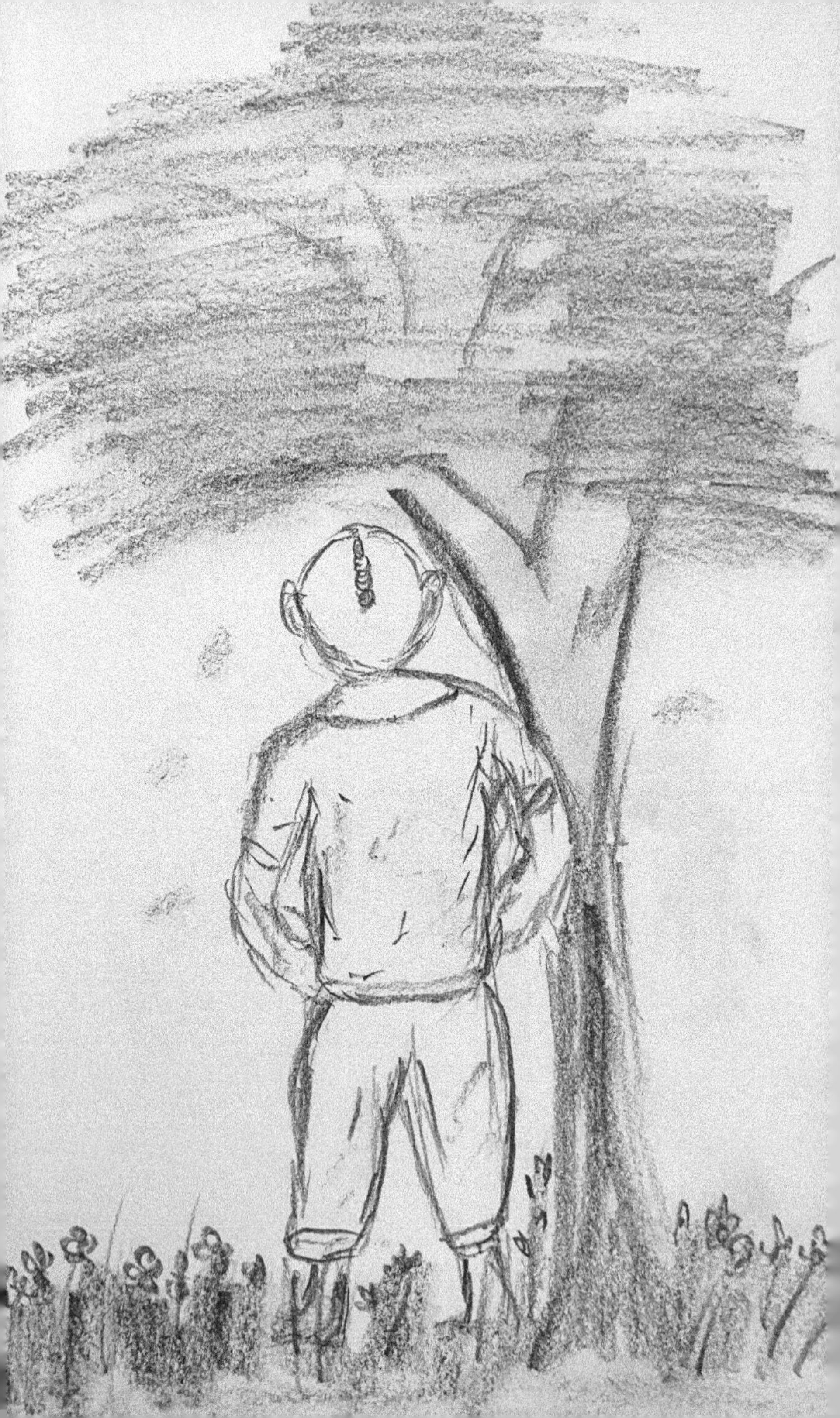

We are all
a work in spirituality,
performing
daily rituals
religiously,
waking up
with the clock,
coffee,
brushing teeth,
bath,
breakfast on the go,
stress on the forehead,
conversations,
inside the head,
brisk walk to
car,
dedicated work hours,
end of shifts,
performance upbeat,
sleepless nights
and
sleeping
with the clock,
next morning
performing
the same ritual,
day after day
We – the dedicated
working spirituals

As they walked further, Amoor saw a parcel of paddy fields not too far away. A couple of makeshift shelters jutted out, their roofs covered with palm leaves, they looked old and worn out yet functional. The two reached near a tree under which an older man was resting on his straw mat. The area beneath was evenly plastered with mud and decorated with some colorful figures.

"Thank goodness, there is someone else in sight too," whispered Amoor to himself, with a sigh of relief.

Seeing them, the old man quickly got on his feet. With folded hands, he bowed with great reverence to greet the two. In response, Sensei bowed too. The way they greeted each other showed immense respect as well as familiarity between the two.

Amoor was a stranger to this kind of greeting and, while still wondering what to do, said, "Hello!"

The old man smiled widely and dramatically opened his arms. In a very welcoming loud tone, he said, "Hello, Sir! My name is Kopi. Welcome to our village!"

"Master Kopi, here, we have a guest today! Perhaps to learn something from our knowing of life so far!"

"And he has a chance to discover himself too," Kopi added with excitement.

"Discover ... didn't Sensei say that too?" A thought flashed in Amoor's mind, but he was too preoccupied to make sense of these statements. He didn't even try.

"Master Kopi, my friend here has a full day of travel today! Before we go for a walk further, may I leave him with you for some time while I get some water," requested Sensei.

"Sure, Master! In the meantime, our guest can rest here his tired feet," replied Mater Kopi, looking at Amoor's bare feet.

Sensei took leave of them and briskly walked away.

"Sir, you are blessed to be in the company of Master Sensei. Please relax, and if you wish to lie down and rest under the tree, I have an extra mat here and an extra pair of slippers," Master Kopi motioned with his eyes and hands.

An old handwoven brown bamboo mat with soft blue lining was resting, rolled up, against the stem of the tree. A pair of slippers were lying beside the bamboo mat.

"Umm … thank you," stammered Amoor and, hesitatingly, stretched open the mat for his seating and slipped his feet in the slippers. The size was just right. "Did he know that I would need footwear?" thought Amoor but resisted asking.

His feet felt very comfortable and rested in those old-style slippers.

"Master Kopi, may I ask you a question? You just addressed Sensei as Master. He is just a little boy! Is this the way you talk to people here?"

"Hahaha!" Kopi laughed aloud. His uneven teeth seemed to be dancing in mirth. "No, no, we don't address everyone as Master, Mr …?"

"Oh, Amoor, my name is Amoor."

"Yes, Amoor, so I was saying that we don't address everyone as Master. Sensei is very special. Long before he was born, the people of this village used to come to me for all kinds of advice. I am a life reader by birth. I am blessed with this gift that I can see anyone's probable future. Knowing my capabilities, people started calling me Master. When Sensei was born, I went to bless him, and the moment I looked at him, he smiled. There was an unusual glow and wisdom on his face. I could tell that he was a highly evolved soul. Right away, I named him Sensei, which means the Master. So, he is a Master of a master! And I wasn't wrong. He is one of us, but his wisdom is that of a sage! Now, the whole village seeks his advice and covets his company. You may have experienced that already," concluded Kopi with a smile on his face, which was crisscrossed with wrinkles of decades of experience.

"Of course," muttered Amoor. "It is, indeed, unbelievable! I've never met anyone like him before! You know what I mean. Sensei is irresistible … I got glued to him within minutes and followed him all the way here. I still can't understand what's going on. I was actually thinking …"

"Amoor, how about giving your mind and body some rest. You must be tired," Kopi said gently, "Don't think too much. You are on your way home. *If life alters your plans, remember it has something better for you. Try not to take control of it. Let life happen!*"

"Why did Kopi say that? Does he know my thoughts or about my life?" rattled a bit, Amoor questioned to himself. A frown appeared on his forehead as he pondered more.

Lying on his straw mat, Kopi started humming a song in a melodious voice, "The breeze blows … la la la … the water flows … la la la … but my soul … oh my soul … always glows … la la la …"

"It is ok to smile," Kopi paused and looked at Amoor with a twinkle in his eyes, interrupting the seriousness on his face. "Just a silly old song, singing for fun!"

A big smile appeared on Amoor's face upon hearing this. He laughed despite himself. His cheeks felt a little stretched and red as a rush of fresh blood flushed them up – he hadn't laughed often. He felt a lightness in his chest. The sound and feeling of laughter felt good to him. These are interesting people! And he felt an urge to laugh and laugh and laugh …

A frame
called body
catches my soul
from escaping
otherwise
I am
simply
non-existent

The Knowing

After some time, Sensei returned. With a beige cloth bag on his shoulder and a clay pot on his head, he walked like a juggler, trying to balance. As Sensei walked, the water spilled out of the clay pot. Seeing this, Amoor smiled mischievously like a kid.

"Sensei, I think most of the water has already spilled!"

Sensei rested the pot under the tree, supporting it with a couple of stones at its base.

"Oh yes, Amoor! The pot is, indeed, half-empty!" Sensei replied mischievously too.

"All that walk and hard work for nothing, huh!" Amoor couldn't help saying.

"You may be right, Amoor. But wait, I'll show you my magic!" said Sensei excitedly. He took a small transparent glass bottle out of the bag. The pinkish color of the liquid inside made the bottle look pink in color. Sensei pulled open the tiny cork cap of the bottle.

"What is it?" asked Amoor as his nostrils filled with the fragrance of the aromatic drink.

"This is sweetened milk with honey and extract of rose flowers," Sensei replied.

"Aabra ka daabra … mix … mix … blend … blend," Sensei giggled and mixed the pink liquid into the pot.

Then he poured the drink into two clay mugs that Kopi had produced from a basket lying beside him. Sensei offered that refreshing drink to Amoor and Kopi.

"Ahhh! This is delicious!" exclaimed Amoor. He had never tasted anything like this before. The color, the aroma, the taste … just overpowered him.

After taking a few sips, Amoor looked at Sensei and asked, "But, Sensei, what about the magic you were talking about?"

"Oh, yes, the magic! The magic here was a wonderful life lesson."

"Life lesson? And what was that supposed to be? I didn't notice anything special happening. All I saw was the half pot of water!"

"That emptiness of the pot was the magical lesson, my friend. Did you notice that when the pot became half-empty, it created room for me to add something else in it?"

"Yes, I did. That's how it is, anyway. What about it?"

"Because the pot was half empty, I was able to add that delicious liquid in it. I kind of like this process. It tells me *that if we keep letting go of what we have already filled, we always have room for new and more to come. What is full can never be filled again.*"

"I see …"

"And, look, Amoor, the spilled water helped nourish the grass and the plants too. What I let go can be used somewhere else. Your learning, your knowing can be utilized by someone who needs it. It is a recycling world. You empty and fill and empty and replenish till you intuitively understand this is the process of life."

Amoor nodded his head. He drifted into deep thought after hearing the concept of being empty and being fulfilled for the first time. He took a deep breath, got up from his mat, and walked a few steps with arms crossed, still dwelling. Without looking around much, he walked towards a big rock and seated himself quietly on the precipice of that big stone under the vast expanse of colorful sheets of the sky, reflecting on what Sensei had just said. His ruffled hair had gathered some dust with the movement of the day's events. His hand reached his jaw, expecting to run his fingers through the peppery beard. He got startled. His morning dream was mixing up with what was happening now. It felt like déjà vu!

"Good heavens! This is so similar to the dream that I had this morning," he said to himself, surprised and feeling confused. "Is the dream becoming alive?" he asked himself in disbelief.

In his daily life, Amoor was always full of knowledge, confident of his opinions, and sure that he understood everything pretty well. But, the unexpected happenings of the day put him on a shaky ground where everything was open to a new interpretation. His heart had started to connect with his lost spirit. New episodes of questions and possible answers sprouted up like buds in the freshness of the spring. It was the beginning of a journey to his inner self, the journey of the opening of a new path from the head to heart, a journey from a pseudo-identity he had donned to an authentic self he had forgotten. Of course, it was unsettling to begin with. But this was the moment of truth.

"Are these events trying to give me a message? Have I always been a full pot?" he thought gravely. "And perhaps that is why no plants ever bloomed in my life. Nobody has stayed with me happily or for long. I, perhaps, never watered my relationships. Is this what I am supposed to understand?" Amoor suddenly spoke aloud, throwing up his arms in restlessness.

Amoor's flustered expressions did not go unnoticed. Kopi got up at once to soothe his agitation and patted his back. Amoor couldn't resist that loving fatherly affection. Like a child, he put his head on Kopi's fragile shoulder. His eyes welled up with tears, and sobs heaved his once hard and proud chest. He didn't even understand why he broke down like this. Perhaps it was time to let go and become empty to allow room for new to flow in.

"I know how it feels, my child," said Kopi softly, as he embraced Amoor in his arms and stroked his head.

"Here, please have more," said Sensei as he offered Amoor more of the delicious drink.

FLOATING EMPTY

The world I built
with presence of my own
my own living
my own words
my own thoughts
my own doings
is now old and
rickety
Needs minimalism
needs emptiness
to become new and
open to life
that I have not
lived yet
So far I was
living in the same
house I built
years ago

The Connection

Amoor, Kopi, and Sensei sat together for a while. No one spoke anything. The only sound that could be heard was that of the water flowing over the rounded stones in the little creek. Once in a while, a couple of parrots squawked and hopped around the curvy branches of the mango trees. This sight took Amoor back to childhood memories that had become hazy with time.

"Did you ever try to climb a tree when you were a kid, Amoor?" Sensei broke the silence while looking at a mango tree.

"Err … yes, I did."

"Then share something with us, too, from your childhood!" exclaimed Kopi.

"Hmm … I wasn't that good at climbing trees, and, one time, I almost broke my ankle!" Amoor almost giggled but managed to do with a smile as he traveled back to his childhood. "All my friends laughed at me when I fell on the ground, but that is how it was – we did silly pranks. We laughed, fought, cried, and celebrated small successes. I remember my friends once lifted me on their shoulders and carried me home when I first climbed a very tall mango tree." Amoor looked happy to travel back in time to those good old days.

"Yes, it is a great feeling to be with our friends!" exclaimed Sensei, with exuberance. "Do your friends still celebrate the small stuff'?" he asked.

Amoor suddenly looked serious.

"No! It's been a while since we parted ways."

"Why? What happened, Amoor?" asked Kopi.

"What do you mean by what happened?" Amoor asked with a slight tremor in his voice.

"You said it has been a while …"

"Uh," Amoor's lips curled down. "Many reasons …" he said, his voice lowering down to a whisper. "Someone became egotistic, someone was too busy with career and family, someone moved away or just drifted apart."

"That's not fair. Are you sure you are not one of those someones Amoor?" Sensei's question had a hint of probing in it.

Amoor's forehead frowned again at this question. "What do you mean?"

"Let it be Amoor, perhaps it makes you uncomfortable," Sensei calmly replied.

"No, no, I mean … yes… well … alright, tell me what you mean?" Amoor stammered.

"Amoor, we are very accustomed to justifying ourselves by blaming others. Seldom does anyone say – 'I could have been better myself … that was not completely the other person's fault.' Right?"

"Huh?"

"When we've friends and family, we automatically assume that they should understand us, they are answerable to us and should get along with us. In all relationships, unconsciously, what we don't say but assume and expect is that the relationship should be on our terms."

"In actuality, I don't understand what happened between us. My friends made no effort."

"If your friends did not make an effort, did you do? If they became egotistic, did you drop your ego to embrace them? It is not about staying connected to everyone all the time. It is about understanding that others may have something going on in their lives too. Each person is trying to make the best of life wherever they are. In the course of that, if they can't connect to you, maybe you can reach out to them."

"We just went our ways, never looked back," Amoor shrugged his shoulders.

"Maybe you could have attempted to understand their side of the story. Listen, relationships are not easy to build and are also hard to bear when they break. People love to stay connected to those who are willing to let go of their rigid beliefs or set ways of thinking. Your ideas, your beliefs, your truths, your knowing are yours only and not someone else's. In friendship, you have to know your friends, understand them," saying this, Sensei paused.

"Hmm ... I get that part, but ... please go on."

"Amoor, what we have already mentally accumulated is an old story. Embrace the new ways; life is fresh every moment — welcome other's ideas and opinions. Have room in your life to be open to the new, the unexpected. Do you understand this?"

"Umm ... how does this relate to my relationships?"

"See, two things are very significant. One is flexibility, and the other is adaptation. It is not very difficult. In a garden, become a gardener, with a child become a child, bright with the sunlight, wet with the rain. What are you protecting all the time? Your ego? You are not opening your heart to anything or anybody. Unconsciously, you want others to be just like you – think like you, live like you. That's how you accept them. If they don't, you break up your relationships with them. Is your way of living the only correct way? No, not at all. Universe has created diversity in myriads of ways. Things may appear to be similar in some ways but are never the same. When any two forms blend, a completely new, unique form takes place. Living our own way in the same manner, with the same ideas, same rules, and regulations, is nothing but a repetition of our life. Loosen up and see how life changes for you. Be at ease. Empty your pot, Amoor. Free yourself from the concepts of what I know, what I am, what I believe in. We all exist together as a part of the Whole."

"So, should I not be myself?" a question slipped from Amoor's mind through his lips aloud.

"I see you have a lot of attachment to your identity. You don't have to be what you already are —yourself. You can be yourself AND let others be how they are. Try to accept and embrace the differences of others wholeheartedly. Everyone is as important as you are, Amoor. If you can absorb what I said, many of your relationship issues will be solved," Sensei calmly rested his words.

We all are colors
yellow face
of fear,
red of
anger,
white of
being caught,
pink of blush,
grey of hair,
like
red of sun,
white of waves,
grey of clouds,
pink of flowers…
colors in us
prove
how we
are a fragment
of
universe
yet
carrying
whole
in
us

The Mantra

Every time Sensei spoke, an incessant flow of wisdom seemed to float in the air. The only interruptions were thoughts of Amoor. His mind had as many question marks as could fit in his head. A lifetime of the practiced behavioral pattern was not easy to break. The repetition of the same response and often the same reaction had now become a part of his personality.

In a little edgy tone, he shot back, "Are you saying the problem is with me?"

Sensei looked at Amoor as if looking past his persona, got up from his place, and gently held his hand in his tiny hands. "Amoor, the world is a beautiful place. You just have to see it with fresh eyes. You want to be yourself, that is well and good, but while being yourself, you also add something else in your living. That changes the equation."

"And what is that, Sensei?"

"Control."

"Control? Where do I control in relationships? I don't! Work? Yes, I do!"

"You will be surprised that you are not the only one who is unaware of this facet of daily life. Almost every relationship has one person who takes the upper hand and takes command. This control mechanism can also be so subtle that it becomes hard to describe it. It is basically forcing others to live your way. Control may appear in many forms."

"Such as?"

"Control is when someone shouts and screams when others disagree or won't act as you want them to. Becoming silent and sullen to show disapproval is also control. You will be surprised to know that control can also be by way of self-pity."

"Self-pity is control? How does that work?"

"People who cannot control by power may go into self-pity. They may create a self-image of a victim. They try to feel good by sharing exaggerated stories of their own self-sacrificing efforts and blaming others for not reciprocating or labeling them as ungrateful. They gain sympathy this way. It is an attempt at empowerment in a twisted way, and that creates an indirect pressure on others to force them to act in a certain way. Even the seemingly weakest can exercise control in not so obvious ways … the list goes on and on. We use unhelpful ways to find helpful solutions! Anyone insecure tends to exert control to feel a sense of security."

"That's very interesting to know. I'm surprised, I thought only the powerful have control issues."

"To take it into a day to day scenario, Amoor, tell me, how would you feel if you always have to plan and think before you talk to your family or friends in order not to get them upset?"

"I … umm …"

"You won't like it, right? Then why would your friends, your family, have to think twice before talking to you?"

Sensei's grilling remark left a visible impact on Amoor. He dug his toe in the soil with his head down, perplexed at how much Sensei knew about him.

"And, Amoor, please don't take it as a personal criticism. This is just a part of your learning," added Kopi with a lot of kindness in his voice.

"Oh, no, I'm not taking it personally. In fact, I'm indebted to Sensei for teaching me these invaluable lessons. I've lived and suffered the hard way, and I'm open to learning!"

"Reflect on what is being said here to you today. Try not to judge those people whose behavior is not in tandem with yours. Practice empathy" continued Sensei.

"Huh, I've heard of empathy. What is it exactly?"

"Empathy is all that we have just talked about. Understanding others with compassion, acknowledging their pain and sorrows, encouraging them to express themselves so that they too bloom. Start with these."

"Hmm ... I think I've some clarity now. What else?" said Amoor deep in thought.

"Nature has a lot to teach us. Learn from the rhythm of nature. Look around here, the bees, the ants, the birds, the river, the trees … look for a moment," Sensei paused as he looked around. "Do you see anything interfering with anything else? Are they all behaving in the same manner? The bee collects honey, and the birds don't. The river flows, and the trees are stationary. But they all are existing together. This variety of life is what has made existence possible. Nature has designed us to be different and be accepting of each other. The sun, the moon, and the stars all prevail in the same space even though their energies are completely different. All exist as is – in unison. Just like an orchestra with different instruments playing but creating one harmonic symphony. And where is the magic of it all? The magic is in your connection with your heart." Sensei's last statement had a full stop in it.

But Amoor's head was still racing. He had so many questions that needed to be answered.

Without wasting any time, he quickly asked Sensei, "How do I know whether I am in the heart or the head?"

"It is simple, Amoor. When you are in your thoughts – calculating, analyzing, judging, looking at your own sole benefit, even at the cost of others – you are in mind, in the head. When you are simply loving, giving out of love and compassion, when you are in joy – you are in the heart. Being in the heart will feel like you are in the womb – you are like a child again, trusting, safe – in the care of the Universal Mother from where all life flows. You'll know it … in fact, you know it, and we all know it. Use the mind for day to day practical activities and use the heart for everyday interactions with the people, the birds, the animals, with all sentient nature."

Sensei became silent after this. The sun, like a mural in the backdrop, blended with the white floating clouds, lending them a pink dash. It felt as if the time had come to a standstill listening to Sensei's words.

For the time being, Amoor did not say a word. He just sat motionless, eyes closed, as if in a trance. A flashback of his entire life and relationships ran like a movie inside his head. A few tears trickled down his face and fell on the ground below. One black ant made an appearance from its hiding place and hurried back again.

Let it grow....

My existence is
in multiples
one character
many roles
trying to live
one by one
expectations
of the world,
when will
they break
the shackles
around my
expected identity
and set me
free to
bathe in the
brightened
glory of
me
being me

The Healing

Nearby, in some muddy puddles, a few pinkish-white lotus buds floated sitting on top of their flat green leaves, glistening with rays of the sun piercing straight through the clouds. The unopened petals of the lotuses quivered with the gentle movement of the breeze. Amoor looked intensely at this act of nature and felt the yearning of buds to open and bloom, similar to the way he was feeling.

"Ahh … it feels so different from my daily life," he whispered very softly.

He had kind of forgotten to share or talk about how he felt inside. He realized that he had started living in a shell, withdrawing into himself as life brought different experiences. He had constructed mental walls around himself so that no one would access his feelings. He kept love at bay and firmly dealt with the world so as not to be perceived as weak. His definition of himself had entirely changed from when he was young.

"And when did this happen?" he asked, his mental conversation with himself sprouting one more time as he looked at thirty-plus years of his life. The fountain of joy in his heart had languished. He felt he had paid a heavy price for his success.

His moments of introspection were soon over. He saw Sensei getting up and slipping his feet in his wooden slippers.

"Master Kopi, we'll take leave of you now. There is a lot to explore today with my friend, Amoor. Let's go, Amoor."

Amoor nodded in agreement.

Sensei bowed to Master Kopi with folded hands. Kopi smiled and placed his right hand on Amoor's head affectionately. Amoor's eyes instantly moistened as if a child was separating from a parent. He folded his hands too, closed his eyes, and bowed the way Sensei did. At that very moment, he felt that all thoughts in his head had utterly vanished. There was no sound, no sight, no trepidation, just silence. That one moment of eternity gave his mind tremendous rest.

"Amoor," whispered Sensei, "Bowing with a heart full of warmth and gratitude is a wonderful form of surrender. My friend, you are a new person today. Those who learn to surrender open their hearts to life's many gifts. Let's go!"

Amoor gave the slippers back to Kopi and put on his shoes again. They didn't seem to hurt anymore.

What an amazing day! Amoor had opened his heart to a new relationship. He had surrendered his ego before Sensei. Age did not matter. What mattered was that he had opened the "door" of his "house" to let someone in. From his ever talking and calculating head, Amoor had made a new corridor to his heart again. Yes, again.

I am synonymous
with life
which never ends
in spite of all upheavals
it regenerates
Water crawls and meanders
and permeates mountains
finding its way
and its survival
Plants sprout
cracking the solidity
of rocks
Trees spring
back after fall
unfolding the
hidden greens
Life keeps going
on and on
and me too

The Love

"Sensei, I feel the way when I was young …" Amoor felt energetic after resting. He had a new spring in his walk.

"You are still young!" interrupted Sensei with a chuckle.

"Yeah, I mean, when I was in my twenties, I fell in love with Piu. My heart feels the same today – free, clear, excited, and unburdened. I feel as if life has gone back to those days," said Amoor with a deep relaxed breath.

"Really?" Sensei initiated to know more.

"Piu is forever in my heart, but she is not in my life anymore." As soon as Amoor said this, numerous waves of past memories ran up and down his face. He quickly tried to recover from the impact of this revisit to an aching chapter of the past.

"I would like to hear your love story, Amoor, the thought of which had brightened your voice. Let's talk as we walk. How did you meet her?"

Amoor's voice shook when he tried to speak again, "Sensei, I met her on a day when I was running late for an interview. When I reached the office, I was directed to an office where I was supposed to submit my documents. There, seated behind the desk, was this young woman who greeted me in a cheerful voice. I felt an instant attraction towards her, not because she was beautiful but because her calming voice and welcoming smile put me at ease. She introduced herself to me as Piu. She read through my papers quickly. Her glance at me, the slight tilting of her neck, moving her hair back from her face – all these gestures are still captured in my heart. At that time, I had no idea that I would fall in love with her, that I would love her more than anything else in this world," paused Amoor to catch his breath as he narrated the first meeting.

Sensei could hear the pounding of Amoor's heart. "Please go on. This is quite interesting!"

"She said that they had almost finalized a candidate, but she would try to get me interviewed. Once again, I was captivated by the kindness of her voice. In a soothing voice, she said, "Life always gives us our share of happiness, it just happens. If this job is for you, you'll get it." I got that job. Her trust in life was complete. That day was my first introduction to trust. Later, I went back to thank her, but she had left for the day. On the first day of my new job, I went to her office to see her. To my surprise, I found out that she worked in my department."

"Over a few weeks, she fell in love with me. I, of course, was already in love with her. Her way of life was very different. She always gave a positive spin to even the most difficult situations. Her eyes had the peace of the sky and the depth of the oceans. Sometimes, she laughed like a child, very innocent, and, at times, she was like a teacher, very wise. She was adaptive, flexible, as you say, Sensei, she was like water – clear, flowing, and nurturing. There was something special about her, something serene. It seemed like she had a charisma, which was hard to define but easy to feel. She lived life in the moment! Love made us inseparable."

"Hmm ... Did you get married to her?" Sensei asked.

"Ahhh," Amoor sighed heavily, "I wish I did." Amoor stopped and turned his face away.

"Why, what happened?"

"Sensei, I can't explain what happened. I couldn't have asked for more from life. But, at that time, perhaps, it was my young age or immaturity or fear of taking responsibility … maybe I was not mentally strong to make a decision …" Tears welled up in Amoor's eyes as he journeyed back. He seemed wistful and forlorn.

"Ohh … I'm sorry. You don't have to talk about this if it feels so painful," Sensei looked at Amoor quizzically.

"No, Sensei, I need to vent it out. Please bear with me." Amoor's voice was emotional. He continued, "As I said, we were very much in love. When I told my family about us, they disapproved of it. They thought that she was way down in social and economic status compared to us. They saw marriage as an opportunity to move up in society, but certainly not to go down. My family threatened to outcast me if I married her. I was willing to leave my family for the sake of Piu, but she insisted that I should not. She said I would start missing my family after a while, and that would be a huge stress on our marriage. I was torn inside and was getting depressed to the extent that I started drinking excessively to forget my woes. I met her less to avoid the pain, which, in turn, hurt me even more. Her ever-happy eyes seemed to struggle to catch up with the smile she put on her lips. The pressure from my family to leave her was immense. It was tough … very tough. It was impossible to imagine life without her. I suggested to Piu that we get married and later on, I'll tell my parents. She wasn't so sure to start her new life like this."

"I think she followed ethics in life and did not find it appropriate to hurt your parents for her happiness. Then?"

"Then, one evening, Piu called me to meet her at the bank of a stream where we often used to meet. I can never forget that evening. The dusk had fallen. The darkness was enveloping the landscape. Dark clouds rumbled in the sky. The moon had come out in a big white orb. It was a full moon night. When I reached there, Piu was sitting on the river bank, wearing a long white cotton dress. From a distance, she felt like a reflection of the moon on the grass. On seeing me, she got up and ran towards me as if I was her lost treasure. She wrapped her hand around my hand so passionately as if never wanting to leave it. I felt a deep pang inside my heart – I intuitively felt that something drastic was about to happen. My heart thumped so fast and loud. I could barely take my eyes off her as I caressed her hair. We sat together, holding our hands. I asked her if everything was alright."

"Amoor ... I've to say something," she stammered for the first time.

"What is it?" I asked her, looking at her sad face.

With a cracking voice, she said, "You are everything to me, Amoor, my world, my life, my love. I can't see you in pain anymore. Love is meant to understand, give, bring happiness. How can I let my love for you see you get hurt like this? These days you've lost your smile, your peace, your health. My love is immense and not selfish. I cannot be the reason to bring to ruin your life or separate you from your family. This is it, Amoor ... this is it!"

"What do you mean? What are you saying, Piu? Everything will be alright." My heart sank with the foreboding of a separation from her.

"I've decided to move back to the town where my parents live. I won't be meeting you anymore, nor should you try to connect to me. You are a part of my existence now, and you will remain in me, in my memories, in my prayers, forever. I am very grateful that I could experience your love. Not very many people are so blessed to give and receive love. But our journey together ends here, Amoor … it ends here!" Piu couldn't say anything after this. She started sobbing uncontrollably.

"Shocked at what she had just said, and the finality of her decision, my heart was going through tumultuous emotions. I felt crushed. I knew she was fighting herself, trying to control her emotions. I touched her wet face with my hands and started crying. All the pain of the previous weeks and months and the anguish of what was about to come broke the dams of my fortitude. It felt as if two souls were being ripped apart from their bodies forever. Soon, it started to rain, and then a heavy downpour followed. The skies too seemed to be unburdening uncontrollably that night with thunderous claps of lightening zigzagging the abyss and lighting up the entire canvass of creation. Hours seemed to pass by as we held each other's hands, tears rolling down our eyes. I tried to talk Piu out of her decision, but she had made up her mind.

She said this was best for her and me in the long term. That was a night of immense turmoil and outpouring of love that doesn't often happen in our lives." Amoor gave a big sigh.

"The rain finally stopped. The dense clouds parted. Momentarily, Piu bloomed into that magical smile and said, "Amoor, I am leaving my love with you and keeping yours in my heart. Your love made me feel so special, so beautiful, always. I love you so much! Promise me that you will take care of yourself!" Saying that, she waved me one last good-bye, tears streaming down her cheeks. I can never forget her last words and her departure from my life. They haunt me. It was a night of partings – two different paths had formed never to meet again ..."

Soul
Connections

22nd April 2020

A flash of memory
intrudes in
our most
eternal vicinity
laced with
immense pain
with an unwarned
attack as always,
hardly realizing
that in any age
no soul
is ever bruised
even when
nailed
all over
by conditions
we resurrect...
we survive
despite the
tsunami of adversities
we rise
we are the phoenix
The One –
The Truth

The Sharing

Amoor did not return from this flashback for a long time. Years of memories were coming back intermittently as tears flooded down his cheeks. He had never talked about this part of his heart out to anyone before. He grew up learning that men are the tough ones, that men don't cry, that men are supposed to be the ones to take charge of life. Amoor was going through a reunion with himself at this moment.

Narrating this incident, he had become oblivious to his surroundings while walking with Sensei. He wiped his face and eyes and noticed that they had reached in front of a small cottage. Amoor did not realize that they had been walking for a long time, and the sun seemed to have shifted its position, leaving a crimson reminder of its life-giving presence.

The cottage was circular, with the exterior neatly plastered with mud. Someone had meticulously painted a net of leaves and flowers with white chalk and lime paste on the outer wall. The short path leading up to the cottage was adorned with equally spaced white and grey pebbles. Yellow and pink hibiscus shrubs were planted on both sides of the pathway, which were laden with abundant flowers. The air was loaded with blended fragrances of blossoming litchi, guava, and mango trees. Amoor's eyes absorbed this presence of vivid colors, various textures, and sheer abundance of the infinite macrocosm.

Sensei motioned to Amoor to wait, stooped under the arched door of the cottage, which was ajar, and disappeared inside. Sensei's every movement now brought inquisitiveness in Amoor's heart. He looked forward to what was next; he felt open and receptive to the unknown.

Soon, Sensei reappeared, followed by a very old woman, stooped to half of her size. Numerous wrinkles on her face appeared to be a map of joys and sorrows and all the experiences she had had in her life. She was wearing a white saree with a broad red border patterned with tiny pieces of mirrors sown symmetrically. A thin necklace of wooden and emerald stone beads adorned her neck. Golden flower-shaped earrings hung playfully from the long lobes of her ears. Her well-oiled and braided silver-white hair were almost touching the back of her knees.

The old woman greeted Amoor with her toothless smile. Amoor smiled back. The woman was holding a woven bamboo basket full of fresh marigold flowers. She came closer, raised her hand, put some yellow vermilion powder on Amoor's forehead, and showered marigold petals on his head. Amoor had never met anyone welcoming him in that manner. But it felt good, very good. His heart was happy.

"Amoor, meet Mother Dara, a wise, sweet lady." "She is abundance in herself!" added Sensei mysteriously.

Amoor folded his hands and looked at Dara carefully, trying to figure out what did Sensei mean by "She is abundance in herself."

Dara motioned them to come in. As they followed, she started clapping her hands and started singing, "Bula Bula … aloha Bula Bula aloha … Kuma chopa … bula Bula aloha …"

Amoor looked at Sensei, who was happily nodding his head with the rhythm of the song.

"What is Dara singing?" asked Amoor out of surprise. It reminded him of Kopi's song.

"Oh, it is a welcome song. She is happy that you have come to her home as a guest. She is singing in her native language now."

"Looks like people are fond of singing here! Feels like a happy land!"

"Good to sing and dance and laugh! Keeps everyone light-hearted!" Sensei added.

When they entered the cottage, Amoor was dumbfounded to see an entire world functioning there. The courtyard in the middle of the cottage was open from the top – there was no roof! Right in the center was aromatic holy basil, planted in an earthen pot, which was again beautifully carved just like the drawings on the wall outside. A faint wave of smoke from a half-burnt incense stick was making its way towards the sky. On one side, there were a few sheep and goats, leisurely eating chopped lush green grass, perhaps their afternoon meal. Sensing some unfamiliar footsteps, they shifted their position on their hoofs, going back and forth and uttering ba … ba … ba … eh … eh … eh… in unison as if happy to see the guests too.

In another corner was a makeshift open kitchen with an earthen stove and twigs of trees and dried cow dung to feed the fire. A small area was engaged for kitchen gardening where purple eggplants, ripe tomatoes, and green chilies were ready to be plucked. Something aromatic was cooking on the stove, and from its fragrance, Amoor guessed that it was rice. In another pot, on the smaller second earthen stove, steam was escaping from below the lid.

"Come, sit here, Amoor," Sensei waived and motioned with his hand towards an old pinewood plank perched on two big stones which served as a bench. Dust of the day had gathered on it. Dara hastily picked up a tiny handmade brush made of sheep wool and cleaned the seat. She seemed to be over eighty years old but was quite agile.

"Amoor, Dara speaks several languages, although she has never been to school. Every time I meet her, I find there is so much more to discover about her, so much to learn just by watching her go about her life. When I come here to visit her, I feel so touched to see how she welcomes me with all her heart, although she has few means. Her face lights up on my arrival as if we are meeting after a long time ... as if she will never get this opportunity again. Her welcome pours love out of her heart. Wait till you enjoy her exquisite food," said Sensei.

Dara briskly picked up a small brass pitcher from the kitchen altar and, as a part of her ritual, sprinkled drops of water on the plastered ground with her right hand. After that, she folded her hands, closed her eyes for a few moments in prayer. Then Dara looked up, murmured something softly that Amoor did not understand. She waved her hands with palms down, blessing the house and the guests who had sanctified it with their coming. Sensei explained to Amoor that the arrival of a guest is considered an opportunity to serve, and it indicated that more prosperity, joy, and abundance were on their way.

Amoor was totally new to something like this and was looking at Sensei to get a clue as to how to act. Dara looked like a magician who was setting the stage before starting her tricks.

"Amoor, Dara is invoking all the elements that we are made of – earth, water, fire, wind, and space. To do so is considered auspicious. While she finishes, let's wash our hands."

Once the ritual was over, Dara and Sensei spread a blue rug with an image of bright yellow sun, with its rays tapering out like flames, on the floor. Dara took Amoor's hand and, with a hand gesture, requested him to sit on the rug. Her hand was soft but had an electrifying touch that gave Amoor goosebumps. Sensei also sat on the carpet.

Dara put three plates and bowls on the rug. Amoor looked at them in bewilderment. The circular plates were made out of broad sal tree leaves. The leaves were stitched together seamlessly with tiny wooden sticks.

"Amoor, don't be so surprised. Everything that you see here has a meaning. These are tree leaf plates. In the fall season, people collect naturally dried and fallen leaves. It needs dexterity, time, and patience to knit them together like this. After we finish the food, these leaves are taken to a little compost corner outside the hut that helps to make fertilizer for the plants. This tells us that whatever we may own, whatever we may have worked for, whatever we create or amass – it is all temporary and changeable."

Amoor listened attentively to this example of the cyclical nature of things.

Meanwhile, Dara poured water in bamboo glasses. In a large round wooden bowl, she brought hot steaming rice cooked with a seasoning of freshly grated coconut sambol and served it on the leaf plates with a wooden ladle. The fresh fragrance of coconut started wafting in the air. Then, Dara poured yellow daal sprinkled with fresh coriander leaves on top of the rice.

Amoor couldn't remember when was the last time that he had felt so hungry just at the sight of food! In his day to day life, everything was time-bound and taken care of. Whether hungry or not, he simply ate at a fixed time, day after day. The expression of hunger had waned away a long time back in his busy life. Today, he couldn't wait to dig into the food. As soon as he was about to eat, he stopped and looked at Sensei.

"Go ahead, my friend. Start eating!" said Sensei reaching for his plate.

"I … umm, I … I'm actually looking for, I mean … forks," Amoor stammered and fumbled with embarrassment.

"Forks! Hahaha!" Dara and Sensei both burst into laughter.

Amoor looked at Dara and again noticed Dara's missing front teeth. He couldn't help joining in the burst of laughter.

"Sorry, my friend, we don't have any forks and spoons here," said Sensei.

"Then how will we eat?" inquired Amoor, smiling. He knew by now that Sensei had a solution for everything.

"We use our hands and fingers to eat rice, let me show you. Look at me – use your fingertips to mix rice and daal and create small morsels," Sensei quipped as he poured some more daal on his plate.

"Why not cutlery?"

"My friend, we are sensory beings – we've senses of touch, smell, sight, hear, and taste. When we touch the food with our fingers, we can feel its warmth and texture before it reaches our mouth. That makes the experience of tasting the food much more natural and enjoyable. We are always in awareness when eating with hands. We cannot be absent-minded. It creates an invisible connection between the food and us. Try it!"

"Hmm." Amoor's stomach was already growling with hunger. The fragrance of the food was prompting him just to devour it.

"Eating while sitting on the floor puts us in touch with Mother Earth. It keeps us grounded."

"Is that so?" said Amoor in a voice as if he was in a reverie.

Amoor looked at the food again, restlessly. His head was buzzing with the desire to put a few morsels in his mouth, but he wasn't sure if it was etiquette to start by himself, without waiting for others.

"Your nose has already done its job of smelling the food and making you hungry. Now let your fingers touch and feel what you are going to eat and see how much you enjoy the food!" Sensei added tantalizingly, looking at Amoor, knowing very well that Amoor was desperate to eat.

Amoor could wait no more! He saw it as a signal to go ahead. He quickly mixed daal and rice with his fingers and gulped them down in a mouthful. The rice felt warm and soft, and the daal dripped down his fingers. Over and over, he scooped up the food from the plate, without looking up, and put it in his mouth. After some faltering attempts, he started getting good at it.

Sensei and Dara smiled, delightedly watching Amoor eating like a kid.

"You seem to be enjoying yourself, Amoor!" Sensei said with relish.

Amoor had indeed started enjoying this new way of eating. A little stream of daal trickled down from the corners of his mouth, some rice had stuck around his lips and even on his nose and cheeks! He wiped them off again and again with the back of his hand. His stomach was having a party, his heart full and satiated.

"Ah, it is so delicious!!!" Amoor finally took a break and exclaimed.

"Yes, it is, my child! I can tell this by the spilled rice on your lap," Dara laughingly pointed out.

Plenty of rice and daal had fallen from his mouth into his lap. Amoor felt happy again, like a child. He did not have to be prim and proper in this new world. Imperfection was the new perfection. He didn't have to keep looking at his watch while eating and wiping his face with a napkin. He didn't have to check his phone and eat at the same time. Amoor was quite moved when Dara had addressed him as "my child." Such kindness here! No rules in this land. No judgment, no criticism, just welcome.

"Dara, I can't thank you enough!" Amoor looked at Dara with such gratitude in his eyes.

"Oh, come on, my son! We work so hard all day throughout our lives for the sake of food. We must enjoy our meals to the fullest."

"I agree wholeheartedly … mmm …" Amoor licked his lips, still enjoying the flavors of the food.

"Yes! The mealtime is a meditation in itself. Pay full attention to it. Be aware of someone's hard work and love that have gone into the preparation of the meal. Be appreciative of you being able to see it, taste it, touch it … the joy of being able to relish the food, the gratitude for all of this together." Dara spoke to Amoor while occasionally fanning him and Sensei with a small fan made of dried leaves. The day had become hot.

Sensei nodded his head with approval. Amoor suddenly realized that Dara had not eaten. He felt a twinge of guilt.

"Oh, what you said is so true, Dara! Thank you so much! But you haven't eaten!" exclaimed Amoor.

"I'll eat after both of you have your fill. I am enjoying watching the expressions of satisfaction on your face!"

Amoor thought how unselfish Dara was and how giving her nature was. He wanted to have some of these qualities in himself as he lived in a world where people were mostly focused on their interests.

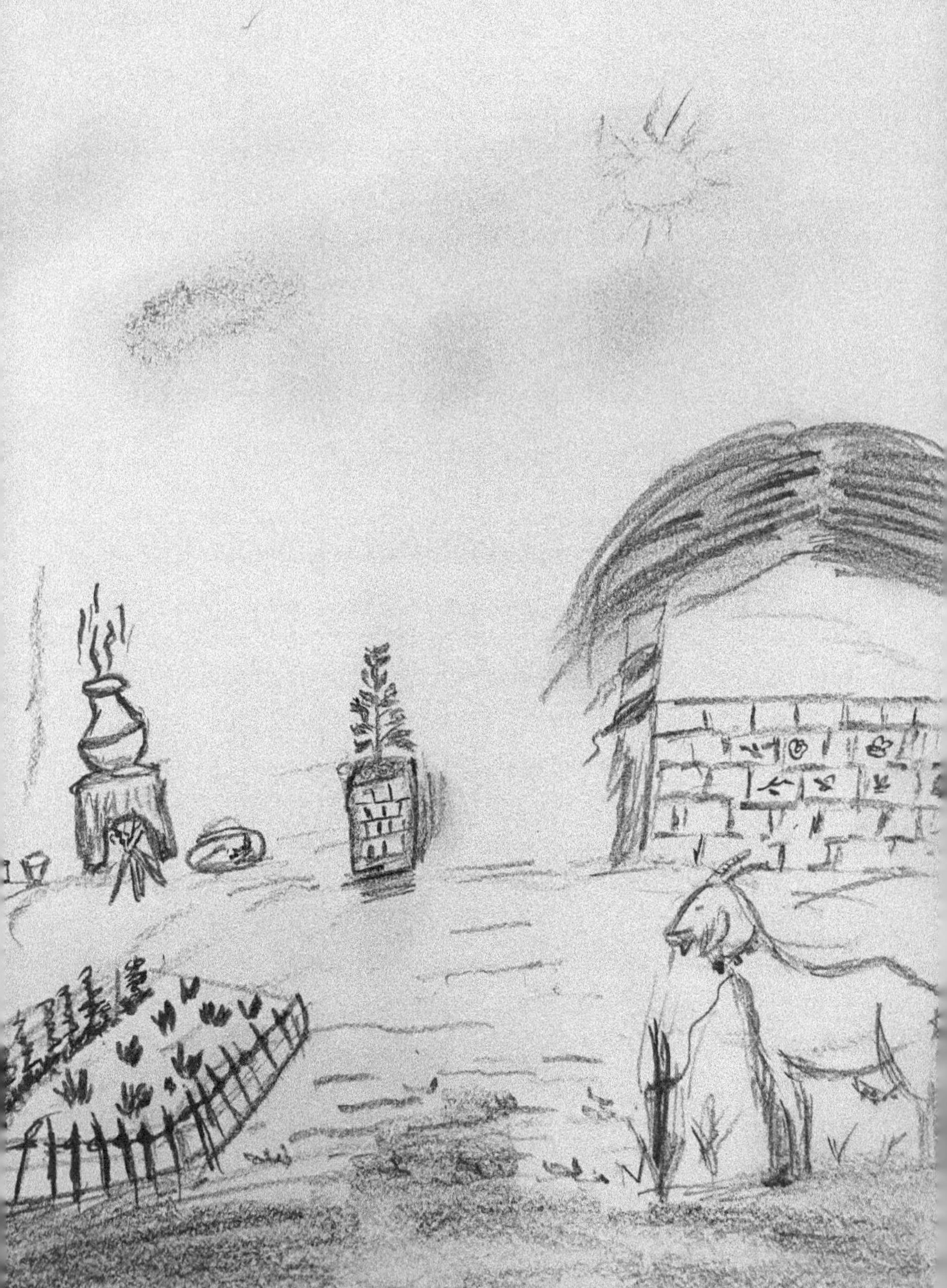

Whispers of my heart
meander through
my mind
looking for
another heart
not head
to blend in
my whispers
and become
one

The Pilgrimage

After they both had finished eating, Dara pulled a little wooden seat knitted with rope and sat on it. She washed her hands and then served food on her plate. Again, Dara closed her eyes for a prayer of gratitude for a few seconds. Deftly mixing daal and rice with her fingertips, she started eating small morsels.

In the meantime, Amoor and Sensei cleared their leaf plates in the compost bins. Sensei took a seat back on the wooden bench where they had sat earlier. Amoor went back and sat closer to Dara. Everyone was silent. The tinkle of the bells around the neck of goats and sheep felt like wind chimes every time they shook their heads.

After Dara finished eating, she quickly cleared the pots and pans from the eating area. Her energetic movements kept surprising Amoor. He yearned to know more from Dara about life.

Dara came and sat closer to him, patted his head with love, and asked, "I see you are lost in thoughts. What is the matter?"

Amoor smiled and said, "Dara, you are so kind and wise. Please share more wisdom from your experience of life."

"Hahaha!" Dara gave a hearty laugh. "This is no wisdom, just simple lessons learned from life. My child, I am so obliged that you have come here, and you have given me a chance to cook and serve you. Ancient scriptures say that way before a guest arrives at your place, their share of food is brought to your home in advance by the universe so that there is always more than enough to feed the guest, yourself, and your family. We should always welcome a guest with an open heart and from a place of feeling abundant. The guest enriches our life. So, you are my reason for abundance in this moment. I am grateful to you for coming!"

Amoor's eyes moistened with tears. Such lessons in humbleness – where else could he have learned what was given to him in this hour!

"Sharing and the feeling of sharing precede many other blessings of life," continued Dara. "Sharing with others not only when you have a surplus but also when you don't have plenty is a magic wand for the heart to blossom. It brings happiness to the receiver and the giver. Sharing does not have to be of objects only. We can share love, joy, happiness, and kindness. But these days, sharing is not all that common. We all try to hold onto what we call 'ours' in this world."

"Right! So, accumulating is no good, eh?"

"It is not just accumulating, Amoor, it is also the attachment to the 'things' and a miserly heart that doesn't allow us to share. Open your heart and see what joy it brings! What did we bring with us when we were born? Nothing! Not even our identity that we identify ourselves with so dearly. Often, I've seen people miserable because they haven't gotten this or that yet, and there is no end to such a chase. Why not spread a wealth of good deeds and fond remembrances while we live!"

"I remember Sensei also taught me about emptiness today. How would that work when we live with our family? I mean, can you say something about family relationships in the context of what you just said. Family life can be quite demanding, I find."

"Amoor, are you married, do you have children?" asked Dara.

"Yes, I am married, and I've two kids."

"How's your relationship with your family, if you don't mind my asking."

"Um … I don't know, Dara. I am quite a busy man, so many things to take care of. I work hard. I have given them a good life, we have all the comforts one hopes for, and … yeah, that's what I do – I'm quite a responsible kind of guy, why?" rambled Amoor, now a little unsure of himself.

"As a parent, you may have told your children many times as to how they should live their life, how to behave, what to eat, what to wear, what to do, right?"

"Of course, I've lived life, and from my experience, I am in a good position to tell them what is right and what is wrong."

"But that was your experience, Amoor, not theirs. It is good to share your expertise of life with them but not force them to be a certain way. They will lose their originality. Didn't you lose yours? Giving them freedom of choice is the greatest gift you can give them. Let your children flower to their potential. Be their guide, be their mentor, be their companion, friend, but don't be their master! The sharing we talked about can be extended to them – share your time and life stories, listen to their stories, share the gifts of curiosity, inquisitiveness. Sharing is the opposite of being stingy, isn't it? Are you giving your family their share of life?"

"Hmm … I share my achievements with them, Dara. I lead by example. They somehow don't like it much."

"Amoor, my child, of course, you are doing everything you can in your capacity for your family. A little but vital thread of connection seems missing. Once you connect the two ends, everything in family life will be seamless. That relentless pursuit of expecting perfection leads to unhappiness."

"Sure, it does, but how do I do that?" reflected Amoor.

"Become a part of their life rather than advocating that how you live is the only or the best way of living. Your experiences and the new experiences of theirs will together create new common ground, a new bond. Accept imperfections as a part of their beingness, your beingness. We are all evolving; no one is perfect!"

"Oh, my goodness, Dara, that's not how I live with them," replied Amoor, feeling quite restless. "I never ask my children what they want to do. Nor do I ask Alie what she wants. Often, I dismiss her choices. I make decisions by myself most of the time and just tell her what to do. What I don't say my expressions do, Alie mentioned once. She knows what gets me upset. Now I know why she said to me one day – I live in your house, but I am absent from your life." moaned Amoor putting his hands on his face.

"Is Alie your wife?" inquired Sensei.

"Yes. I have kind of molded her to live my way of life," muttered Amoor, his voice drenched in little sobs.

"Come here, Amoor, come here," Sensei held him by his arm and took him to the wooden bench to sit on.

"Before you go down the path of self-blame, self-criticism, and guilt, let me explain to you something," said Sensei. "Life runs in a very interconnected manner. It is a deep knit of people, feelings, actions, and learning. Since I met you, I noticed that you often blame yourself. Most of us feel like that when we find out that we could have done things differently. I would say that this a big step in self-reflection. But guilt is very different from self-contemplation. Someone who cannot identify the need for self-improvement leaves no room for inner growth."

Amoor lowered his eyes. A glimpse of his relationship with his wife swarmed past his thoughts.

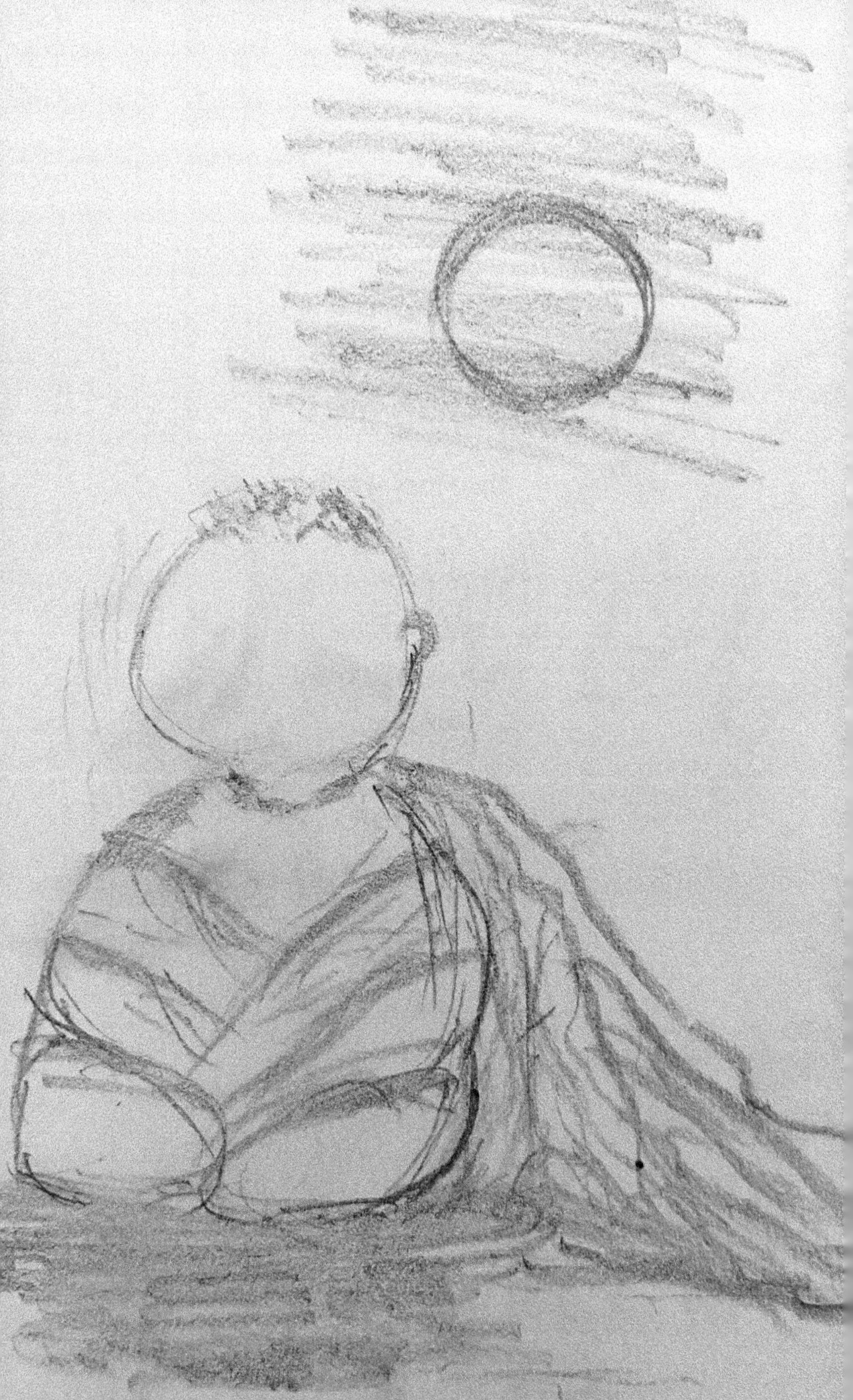

Behind the grey of
my hair
the wrinkles of
my eyes
lives a history
and perhaps
hundreds of stories
of you
of me
and of all
who I know
who now have
hair grey
and wrinkled eyes

The Introspection

For the next few moments, both Dara and Sensei quietly looked at Amoor's face, waiting for him to open up.

Finally, Amoor looked up and then looked away as if not wanting to talk eye to eye. "Alie says something is missing in our relationship," said Amoor reflectively.

"She may be right. Let me ask you something about your past, and we'll take it from there. What happened after you got separated from Piu?" Sensei asked.

Dara was listening with great interest.

"If you don't mind, may I tell Dara who Piu was?" said Sensei before Amoor could answer.

"Sure, go ahead," Amoor replied, and Sensei briefly explained to Dara the part of Amoor's life so enriched by Piu and their sad parting.

"Piu was in each cell of my body. She had become a part of me. After we separated that night, I felt that I had lost myself," Amoor said in a voice choked with emotions. "I waited a day, feeling drained of all energy, and then summoned enough will to go to her house early morning to talk her out of her decision. But … but I was told that she had left the house the previous evening. I spoke to her friends, but they had no idea where she had moved. It seemed that she had disappeared in thin air without leaving a trace of her whereabouts. I know she had kept her promise," Amoor's feelings gushed forth.

"Oh, that's sad," whispered Dara.

"Three years went by, and I hoped that she would contact me one day, my phone would ring, and I would hear her voice. I felt that I could have convinced her to stay with me and marry me. My peace was gone with her leaving my life," Amoor continued, wiping tears.

"Oh, Amoor, my child … you have so much love for her," Dara got up and lightly caressed Amoor's head like that of a little child's.

"Did you find her, eventually?" inquired Sensei.

"No. After three years, I restarted my life. My parents, like all parents, had been worried about me and accepted me with all warmth. But you know, Sensei, this LOVE – once you fall in love, it is so difficult to get out of it. The emotion keeps coming back in some form or the other. I just can't forget her!"

"I can tell from the pain in your voice how much you were in love with Piu. Then what happened?" asked Sensei.

"With Piu as my ever-beautiful memory, I decided to move on. She had always said that she wanted to see me happy. In my heart, I hoped to meet her one day and make sure she was doing well. I've never understood if it was karma or my bad luck, or if she was supposed to come in my life only for a short time and for a reason. I can't understand why we met only to separate. What do you think?" asked Amoor. He looked at Sensei and then Dara to help shed some light and give it some kind of closure.

"Amoor, I'll refer to Piu as your soul mate. Have you heard about this before?" Sensei questioned.

"Umm ... I just know this term, that's it. Never tried to explore its depth."

"Ok, let me explain. A soul mate is someone who feels like the person we have known for a long time, maybe for ages, even though we may have met them for a short time in this life. We may meet one soul mate or more than one in our journey. The purpose of meeting our soul mate and life events is not to bring us pain, although that is sometimes a part of it."

"So, what is the purpose?"

"Life is a constant flow of knowing, learning, and growing. The purpose of soul mates, like other people who come in our lives, is to walk us through different experiences, assist us in exploring our best abilities, reflect on what we need to learn about ourselves and others, and then work on those areas of life. We have to crease out each wrinkle of our experience to move to the next stage of our evolution. These people or incidents or experiences, whatever you may call them, stay with us for a moment, for hours, for days, and some are with us for the rest of our life."

"Then why do they leave us?"

"We may think that they were just chance happenings – that they left us and went their way. In reality, once their role-playing in our lives is done, they prompt us to move to the next phase of life. Pain is what you felt when you parted from Piu. Pain can become suffering, but we should avoid suffering as it serves no useful purpose. We should not become slaves to the memories of the events. It is all a matter of how we view happenings. Our perspective is all that matters."

"So, what should I make of this meeting and parting with Piu?"

"In your life, Piu came to walk you through the chapter of unselfish and unconditional love. Without knowing her, you would have never known love in its true form – giving."

"Did she also have to learn as my soul mate?"

"Yes. Piu had to learn to be empty of that love when the time so demanded, and I am sure life will again enrich her with love. Separation from you made her understand the pain of others. She loved you immensely, and from that experience of yours, you should have become an explosion of love. You should have passed it on to everyone who came into your life. On the contrary, you closed yourself completely."

Sensei paused to see if Amoor was absorbing what he was saying, or he was lost in his emotions.

"Should I continue, Amoor?"

"Yes, yes, please," stammered Amoor, caught thinking again.

"Did you pass on what you had learned from Piu? This memorable experience of love should have been a flow. When your turn came in life to shower love on your family, you became miserly. Unintentionally, you searched for Piu in Alie. You started holding back what you had learned once — the free flow of love. This internal drought has made you dry and parched. You rationed your love in fear of losing it. You felt that you'd get hurt again. Perhaps you substituted control for love, strictness for openness. Alie, who is your life partner, got lost in your world of the past. Alie did not get her share of love from you because you did not start afresh. You lingered on with the memories of your past, and she became a continuation of your pain. You did not even realize that you had deprived Alie of her share of happiness. What happened to you was not her fault. She needs your complete presence in her life, not your fragments." Saying this, Sensei paused as he looked at Amoor with deep penetrating eyes as if reading the book of Amoor's past.

Amoor nodded his head. He exactly understood what Sensei had tried to explain to him. This talk had popped up like a mirror reflecting his life story. This moment was a beautiful awakening.

"Is it too late? What should I do now to make up?"

"Love, Amoor, love again as much as you can so that many lives are touched and changed. Love makes everything mellow and sweet. A loving look in the eyes, a loving pat with your hand, a loving gesture, a loving hug, Amoor, this is all that matters. And each time you do it, it makes you kinder. It brings peace. Most importantly – start with your home. Start with members of your family, and extend to the world."

"I will, Sensei! I will follow this. As it is, life is too short."

"If you say it is short — Live it. Don't waste it by overworking, getting mad at yourself and at others, or blaming, hating. Nothing goes with us when we leave. All that remains behind is the memory. A memory of us. Exactly like you have a loving memory of Piu."

"Thank you so much, Sensei. I think I … I've lived all my life in my head. I don't even know where to start afresh or change the old ways."

"My son," intervened Dara, "As Sensei explained, life moves in invisible circles – it reaches a certain point, and the next circle begins. And if you do not learn from your previous circle and start knitting another, soon you will find yourself in a chain of circles. Neither will you be able to let go of the past, nor will you be able to embrace your present. So, begin with closing your circle from the past. Live in gratitude, in appreciation and value the presence of people in your life and accept them the way they are. Live with everyone and everything in harmony. Live it to the best in the moment; the moment that is gone will not return," saying this, Dara got up, her eyes showering love towards Amoor.

"Enough of talking for now. Let me make some jaggery tea for you and replenish ourselves with some sweet energy," said Dara. Her toothless smile enlivened the moment.

"Sure, sure! I love jaggery tea, and I'm sure Amoor will enjoy the new delicacy of our village. And don't forget to add your special touch of cardamom and saffron to it!"

"Thank you, I am grateful," Amoor replied with folded hands.

I am
a rare component
of universe
fleeting and escaping
world's noisiness,
embracing
the solitary life
of a hermit
at times
living in and out
of my own
silent self

The Ease

The fresh gentle breeze added calmness to the atmosphere. The blend of fragrances from the flowers in the courtyard and the aroma of the brewing tea started floating in the air. Amoor was quite impressed with the spectacular upkeep of the plantation around the hut.

"Sensei, today …" Amoor's voice had a touch of satisfaction.

Sensei looked at him and smiled.

Amoor paused, smiled, and continued, "Today I feel in tune. I feel as if the ache in my heart that had settled in forever like a huge stone is melting away. I feel … I feel … good, very good. I feel ... at ease!"

"Ahhh … ease ... that's a beautiful feeling."

"I understand now that life is always trying to strike a balance. Life wants us to move on."

Dara joined in soon. The aroma of the tea was tempting.

"Very nice … Look at you, my child … all that deep talk …" remarked Dara, handing out hot tea to them in clay cups.

"But Mother Dara, I still have some questions," Amoor addressed her as "Mother" for the first time.

"Questions …? The mind always has questions. Let's keep talking while we enjoy the teatime." Dara seated herself, patting Amoor's head.

"Sometimes, I feel that people around me don't really care about me. That's the reason why I avoid being kinder."

"What would you say about that, Sensei?" Dara looked at Sensei in a familiar expectation.

"Amoor, sometimes people bow down to those who are loud and controlling, but they don't really respect or love them. And there are always people in our lives that care for us, value us. If you care about others, it will be reciprocated, for sure."

"Like attracts like. It is your choice. Being kind is not a weakness. Love, sharing, and kindness are what we need most in our lives," Dara added.

Amoor looked intently at both of them and thought what a blessed moment it was to be in the company of such wise souls.

In the backdrop, the sun had formed a big halo, and in its deep white and orange orb, Sensei seemed like a little Buddha. His words lingered in the depths of Amoor's soul, leaving a lasting impression on his mind. Dara was sitting with deep calmness on her face.

Amoor got up suddenly, bent down on his knees, and placed his head in Sensei's feet in reverence.

"Oh, no, no, please don't do this!" said Sensei, quickly wrapping his left arm around Amoor. His small right hand touched Amoor's head as if in blessing.

"Excuse me ... I just couldn't help it. I ... I've never done that before ..." said Amoor, somewhat awkwardly.

"Get up, please ... please."

Sensei held Amoor's shoulders and helped him to sit up.

"Amoor, in our land, this gesture of bowing is considered very sacred."

"Really? I didn't know that. I thought it was a way of respectful greeting or an act to express gratitude."

"Indeed, it is, and it is more than that. We believe that bowing is a form of surrender. When we bow, in that moment … just that moment, we submit ourselves to the higher consciousness: the ego, the so-called 'my-self' drops. We feel humble. You just experienced that."

"Yes … yes, I did … Sensei … for a moment, my mind became still. No thought, nothing … just peace … it was different …"

"Perhaps you have experienced this before too, but never paid attention to it. This stillness – this is what is called Emptiness," remarked Sensei enigmatically.

Like a school going boy, Amoor's face lit up hearing Master Sensei. He felt a shift in his energy.

He enthusiastically asked, "May I ask you something, Sensei? How are you so enlightened?"

"Dara is my guru, my teacher. She teaches me through words but often through silence. I sit with her for hours. Sometimes, no words are exchanged …" Sensei trailed off.

Amoor looked at Dara with new respect in his eyes before turning his gaze at Sensei.

Following these intense pearls of teachings was a period of deep silence. This pause brought everything to a halt. For Amoor, these repeated glimpses of a pause were intriguing. The mind needs rest from continuous episodes of thinking, self-conversations, and reactions. It always does. We forget.

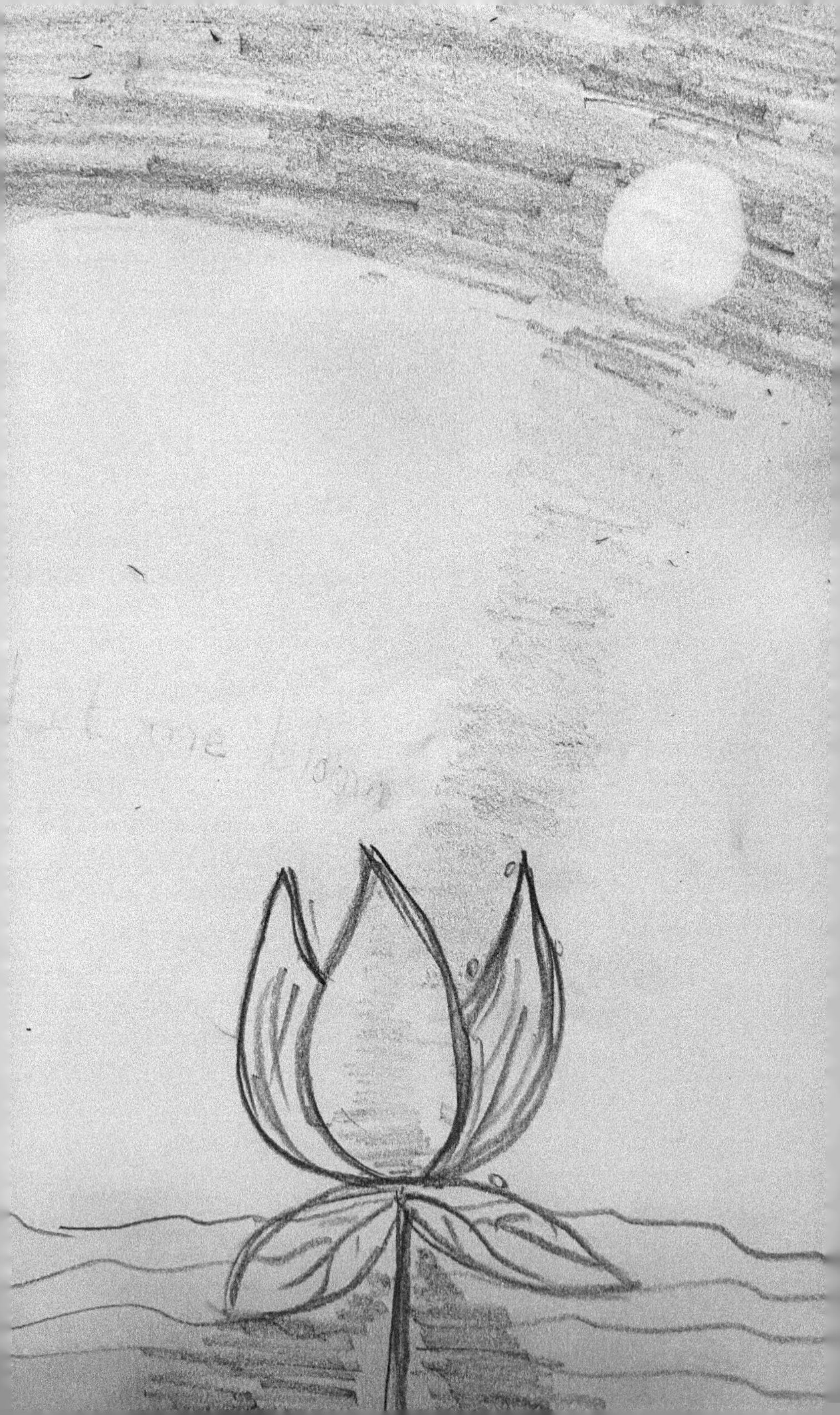

So little knowing of
human nature
and such big
assumptions
of characters,
our own pictures
paint the
people
what they
are
and they
are not
and then
we complain
people
are difficult

The Contemplation

A cuckoo hopped in from the window and melodiously brought everyone back to themselves.

"Ah, this pause felt like a nap!" exclaimed Amoor. Instantly, a thought had reactivated his mind.

"Amoor, drop that thought right here. The mind doesn't have to engage or entertain you all the time. The mind needs conscious rest. Just observe, don't analyze."

Amoor readily received Sensei's suggestion. He smiled back and took a deep breath.

Sensei stood up, folded his hands, and bowed to Dara in the deepest reverence, "Mother Dara, it's time for us to go. Bless us so that we continue to share what we received here today."

Dara smiled, got up from her seat, put her hand on Sensei's head, and then Amoor's in blessing. Amoor again felt the magic of her hand. Time stood still. Farewell, love and best wishes were comingled in that gesture. After a long time, twice in a day, Amoor had felt that ache in his heart when parting from someone. Somewhere inside, he had once again connected and bonded without effort, without reason.

Dara came to the door as they started walking out. When Amoor looked back after walking a little distance, she was still standing at the doorway. She waived and then turned around. Amoor took a deep sigh.

"I'm already missing Dara!"

"I know how you are feeling, Amoor. We would have stayed longer if we didn't have to explore more. This movement – it happens throughout our lives naturally," commented Sensei, explaining that meetings and partings are an inevitable part of life as they walked together.

The well-traveled path was lined intermittently with cedar trees. The dewiness of the wind invited them to walk further. Sensei seemed to know the area very well. He, sometimes, motioned Amoor to step aside from the next little hollow in the ground.

"The world is a very accepting place. It readily accepts and welcomes warmly those who are simple and unassuming, those who are open and receptive and those without an exaggerated sense of self-importance."

"Hmm ... Today is the day when I feel I will receive answers to all my questions. I feel that If I were not my name and status, I would be nobody. I wonder how much people would connect with me without my status," mused Amoor. Turning to Sensei, he said, "Dara had a magnetic persona. I wish I could become somewhat like her. Can I, Sensei?"

"Of course, you can! When you become nobody from inside, that is when you become whole, the biggest magnet in yourself. No effort is required to please the world, no thought of making anyone yours. People get drawn towards you naturally."

"Sensei, to be honest, in my life, relationships have been a big issue. Perhaps, that was my learning in this life. Maybe, that's why all the happenings of the day are leading to that learning. I think I'm, perhaps, able to make sense of all this now. I've always tried hard but was never able to have the bonding that you are talking about."

"Yes, Amoor, all the relationship problems come when we are trying – trying to make things work, trying to accommodate, trying to sacrifice, trying to go out of the way to please. This 'trying' is very short-lived and takes its toll on our mind. Trying is tiring. We cannot keep on trying for long."

"That's so right, Sensei. My mind would never think like that."

"In reality, things are clear, only our minds are muddled."

They had walked quite a distance as Sensei had spoken slowly and took long pauses. His words were gentle, yet had a force. A little farther away, river water shimmered in the light of the sun.

"Wait a moment here, Amoor, and look at that river."

They both stopped briefly. The river water had shades of green and blue and yellow. The sunlight, the flowers on the riverbeds, the trees, the passing clouds – they all had added something of themselves to the colors of the water. On a rounded stone on the bank of the river, a crane stood meditatively on one leg, waiting patiently to have its fill.

"You must have noticed that I talk about water and its magnificence all the time. Do you know why?"

"Nah."

"Water has no color, no shape, no size, and it gives life. Whatever may be the obstruction, water manages to make its way around it. It keeps flowing. The gist, the essence of life ... how to live life can be learned by sitting on a riverbed and watching the water flow. Simply become water."

Amoor breathed deeply. With a new outlook, the world felt like a new place.

Black polka dots
on a scarlet red body
a beautiful countenance…
what's behind this deeper shade?
my love for life,
faith in God,
bonding,
existence
Passion to dream
passion to create
passion to be whole
passion of oneness…
the deep sense of universe
embarks upon me
dressing my being
with
scarlet red color…
Black polka dots
exist side by side,
reminding me
not to forget
the pains, the troubles

I undertook
before transforming into
what I am,
making me realize
difference between
two worlds,
making me...value
my present...
walking happily towards future
I am
maybe
a ladybird

The Enlightenment

After walking along the river for several more minutes, Sensei clapped his hands and waved at someone at a distance. The smell of fish had started to become distinctly strong. From behind an unending row of coconut trees, a thin, elderly boatman raised his hand and waved back.

As they got closer, Amoor noticed an enthusiastic expression on the chiseled and weather-beaten face of the boatman, reclining in his boat. He had a dark complexion, thick grey hair, a small forehead. A bushy, curly mustache added a character to his face. Two thick silver rings hung from his large ears. He had wrapped a green dhoti around his waist, which went down to his knees while his upper body was naked. "He must be in his forties," thought Amoor.

Just like the boatman, the boat, too, had a distinct character – it was tastefully decorated. Several colorful tassels adorned all corners of the thatched hand-painted boat. An old lantern painted in red and gold was hanging in one corner. A wreath made out of coconut leaves and fresh jasmine flowers embellished the center of the boat. The boat swayed gently from side to side with the undulating waters of the river. An old crumpled rope that connected the boat to the wooden stump on the side made a little creaking sound with every motion. The sweeping wind ruffling the coconut leaves added a subtle humming sound to the surroundings.

"Ho Sahib! How are you!" saluted the boatman enthusiastically as he got up from his boat and jumped to the ground.

"All is well, Bodhi," Sensei replied with the same energy. As they walked forward, Sensei briefed Amoor about the boatman.

"This is Bodhi, the boatman. Don't be deceived by his down to earth demeanor. He is a living lesson in himself. The whole village quotes him as a man of wisdom. The rest you will know when you meet him."

Amoor was now ready to receive all offerings that life bestowed. By now, he had become somewhat accustomed to a different walk of life. He understood that each of these introductions that Sensei made had a purpose. A polka-dotted butterfly fluttered around the riverside flowers. Amoor felt the same flutter in his stomach in anticipation of what was to come next.

"Bodhi, this is my friend, Amoor, and he is our guest. I'm sure he will enjoy a ride in your boat if you are happy to offer one," said Sensei hugging Bodhi, who got to his knees, smilingly, to match Sensei's height.

"Sure … sure Sahibji, come my friend, give me your hand and hop on," Bodhi promptly extended his arm. He assisted Amoor to get on the boat by stepping on a few rocks positioned firmly between the boat and the shallow part of the partially submerged riverbed. Sensei climbed on the boat effortlessly as if he had done it many times.

"One minute, Sahib." Bodhi stopped Amoor from sitting.

He quickly picked up a rag and dusted the wooden seats on both sides of the boat. He then carefully opened an old rugged box kept at the bow of the boat. Holding the lid of the box with one hand, he pulled out two beautiful velvet cushions. The cushions, red and gold, were hand-carved using golden sequins with small pearls hanging from the four corners. The cushions seemed new, much to the contrast of somewhat dilapidated boat.

Bodhi placed the cushions on the seats and said, "Now you can sit, Sahib, these are very comfortable to sit on."

Bodhi caught sight of Amoor's admiration of the cushions and proudly remarked, "It's my wife who made these cushions. She is very creative and loves to sew and knit."

Amoor ran his hand on the side of the cushion, feeling the velvetiness, nodded his head, and replied, "Beautiful!"

"Sahib, she also knits lovely shawls, mostly in her favorite colors – red and gold. She says these are the colors of prosperity and good energy," Bodhi said proudly. His voice showed that he was in total agreement with his wife's belief.

"Hmm …" Amoor was new to this concept of color and energy.

"Wait a minute, Sahib, I'll just be back, and then we will sail," saying this, Bodhi jumped out of the boat and ran up the shore.

Amoor looked at Sensei and saw a bemused expression on his face. In the blink of an eye, Amoor saw Bodhi climbing up one of the nearest coconut trees, like a monkey, using his arms and feet with such speed that he was amazed. Within a few minutes, Bodhi came down the tree with four green coconuts tied in a cloth that he had slung around his neck. He returned to the box in the bow and took out a small sharp knife. With practiced precision, he made holes in three coconuts. From his treasure box, he pulled out two clay cups and poured the coconut water in them.

"Here, Sahib, enjoy Mother Nature's refreshing drink," remarked Bodhi jubilantly, offering the cups to Sensei and Amoor, and beaming with a smile. That lifted his mustache a couple of notches.

Amoor noticed that Bodhi had smiled many times as if each little event was an accomplishment. Amoor and Sensei happily received the drink and started sipping, seated comfortably in the boat. Bodhi put the third coconut to his mouth to drink straight from it. Incidentally, it moistened his big mustache. Bodhi wiped his mustache with the back of his hand without any thought or hesitation.

"You got one extra coconut," Amoor couldn't help saying.

"That's for my wife, Sahib," Bodhi said, blushing, and with a twinkle in his eyes.

Bodhi untied the rope of the boat, and with a splash of his ore, started rowing.

"Sensei, where are we going?" asked Amoor.

"Nowhere, Amoor. We are just going with Bodhi … wherever he takes us … with the flow … without a plan, without a destination … just enjoying the ride, the moment … the breeze …" Sensei said in a carefree voice.

Amoor's restless mind became calm on hearing this. It was such a peaceful feeling of going somewhere without a purpose, without an expectation. No worry about the time or making a plan. It felt easy to simply go with the flow. Amoor closed his eyes while he was lost in these thoughts, the damp breeze kissing his face.

Soon his thoughts came to a stop as he heard a melodious sound of a flute. He opened his eyes and saw that Bodhi had set the boat to float and was playing a deep red color flute with golden tassels hanging at the ends. The quivering sound of the flute mesmerized Amoor. It seemed to have a haunting quality to it as if someone was separated from his beloved, yet it was imbued with a tone of warmth. Bodhi played the flute with his eyes closed, completely lost in the music. Behind him was a mural of trees, and the sun was piercing through the gaps of the leaves of the trees, turning waters of the river intermittently into deep yellows and auburns.

"Ah, this is so enchanting … I've never felt this blend of beauty and pain before," whispered Amoor.

Sensei heard him and nodded in agreement. They again got immersed in the world of music and nature's elegant beauty. After a little while, Bodhi stopped playing the flute and took a deep breath. So did Amoor.

"Bodhi, this music was so captivating. What was that streak of pain in your music? It felt as if … as if it had … I don't know …" Amoor was unable to express this blend of feelings.

"Sahib, this music is related to the days when I used to play it for my wife. Whenever I play this flute, it reminds me of my connection with her. It's a long story."

"I would like to listen to it, Bodhi, if you don't mind."

"Oh, sure, Sahib, we all have almost similar stories in our lives. Who knows, my story may have something that you can relate to," said Bodhi with a slight hint of forlornness in his eyes.

"Sahib, this is about a girl I met twenty years ago. Her name is Kokoila, but I call her Koko. I was young at that time, and like most young people who fall in love, I fell in love with Koko. She is stunningly beautiful, not like me … hahaha," laughed Bodhi.

"We soon got married and started living happily. Koko is a wonderful cook. You must taste her special fish infused with hand grounded red chilies and coconut paste and then wrapped and cooked in banana leaves." Bodhi's mouth almost watered at the description of this fish recipe.

"Koko was very creative, resourceful, had many talents, and was happy. She was hardworking and supportive of me all the time. She soon joined me in my coconut harvesting business. We acquired more land, had many more coconut trees, and soon expanded to start a small coconut oil factory. That factory was one of the first here. Therefore, success was immediate. With time, there was more expansion, and with it came more money.

And then something changed." Bodhi's voice became sad. He paused.

"Oh …" Amoor whispered in almost the same tone.

"From everything of ours, the business became mine as I spent more and more time in it. The freshness of love that had existed between Koko and me, and the enjoyment of her presence started disappearing. I had employed more and more people and had started traveling for business while Koko stayed mostly at home. Koko did not seem happy about my prolonged absences and over-indulgence at work. When I reached home after long hours of work, she would wait to talk to me. Slowly, the talks turned to complaints. I used to be too tired after the day's hard work and just wanted to sleep right away. She felt that I wasn't paying attention to her, and I felt that she was too much concerned about herself and did not understand how much I had to work to keep the business running. Most of the time, we noticed irritability on each other's faces and started to avoid talking to each other," Bodhi paused.

"I know how it is, that happens in many marriages," quickly remarked Amoor.

"Oh, no, no, Sahib. I also thought the same – that may happen in many relationships, but it does not have to, it should not. We don't have much of an understanding of how to live, but we think that we do. We think that what 'I feel' is the only valid feeling, what 'I think' is the right thought, what 'I say' needs to be done, what 'I wish' should come to fulfillment. If that is how we want to live, then we should live alone, no?" Bodhi looked at Amoor to see if he understood what he was saying.

Amoor didn't say anything, just listened.

"We need someone in our lives, and then we want that other person to become a copy of ourselves. Why do we need a replica of us in the other person? Why can't we embrace, accommodate, and even celebrate their personalities, characteristics which are different from ours?" Bodhi said all this so fast that he became breathless. He got up from his place, took a few sips of water from his pot, wiped his face with the cloth around his neck.

Amoor didn't know what to say, so he simply nodded.

"That's how things change, Sahib. Relationships that are so precious at one point of time become stale, hard, and even unbearable over time. Often, we don't give enough space to people to live their own lives. We don't make an effort to understand the other, an understanding based on their point of view and not our point of view. It all becomes 'I, me, mine' and not 'you, yours' and most importantly, not 'ours.' That is what happened between Koko and me – slowly, she lost interest in her creative pursuits, her zest for life. She seldom laughed now while she used to laugh at little things before. I lost my appreciation for her. She cooked for us, but I did not look forward to the meals. In fact, I rarely came home for lunch. There were more complaints and now fights between us. Without realizing it, we both put restrictions on each other's lives with our mental lists of likes and dislikes. Earlier, we could talk freely, but later we started keeping to ourselves to avoid quarrels," heaved Bodhi with a sigh.

"That's sad." Amoor's heart felt a connection to the story.

"With time, the distance between us grew more and more. It all looked business as usual on the surface, but there were times when I hadn't looked closely at her face for days. Life became monotonous and predictable. We hardly went out to sit by the river or go to the bazaar or fairs. For me, all days were the same, but Koko insisted on celebrating special occasions or festivals. I sometimes told her that we'd make up for the lost get-togethers when I get time. But you know, Sahibji, the days that are gone are gone. Those moments, those special days or occasions, never come back," Bodhi said with a wistfulness in his voice, his eyes searching for something in the distance. A large eagle flew close over the boat, casting a fleeting shadow and broke Bodhi's reverie.

"What happened then?" Amoor couldn't wait to see how the story unfolded.

"What else Sahib, one day, when it was our marriage anniversary, Koko woke up early morning, wore a beautiful red saree, did her prayers, and lit jasmine incense. She made delicious Kesari dessert with saffron for me. Then Koko came to see me and asked me if we could go out to the bazaar that evening. She wanted to buy fresh jasmine flowers and a few other things to make it a special day. That time I said, sure. Me being me, I got caught up in the day's work and sent her a message that we can celebrate some other day as I'll be busy till late in the evening. Sahibji, that was the last straw." Bodhi stopped and took a deep breath.

He went inside the boat and came out with a piece of roti. He threw the roti on top of the thatched roof of the boat where the eagle was sitting. The eagle picked the piece of roti with its beak and flew away. Bodhi watched till the eagle disappeared into the sky.

"Alright, back to my story. So that day, when I came home for lunch, the house was utterly silent. The food had been cooked, and the fragrance of the basmati rice, aloo-gobi sabzi, and coconut curry, which were my favorite dishes, wafted the home. But there was no sign of Koko. I went from one room to the other searching for her, but she was nowhere to be found. I thought she might have gone to the bazaar, but then I saw a piece of paper with her note on it. She had left me. She wrote that she could not bear to live the pain of loneliness with me anymore, and she had gone to live with her parents forever."

"Oh, good heavens!" sighed Amoor as if Bodhi was narrating something from Amoor's life.

"Yes, Sahibji, that's exactly what I said in that moment too. My heart sank, my lips became dry, and I suddenly felt drained. It was absolutely impossible for me to comprehend life without her. At that moment, I learned how much she meant to me. I realized that I had taken her for granted. You know, Sahibji, in an instant, all my resentments about her vanished. I understood in a flash that my life was nothing without her, that it was her presence that made my days vibrant and lively. The house, the possessions, the wealth – all seemed empty and lusterless. I felt a big void in my heart," sighed Bodhi.

"Bodhi, Amoor too, has suffered the pangs of guilt. Tell him about the happy ending," remarked Sensei.

"Oh, yes … yes, I kind of got lost … it still pains me when I think of it," said Bodhi. Then he continued with revived enthusiasm.

"You know, Sahibji, even though I couldn't wait to see her again, my ego did not allow me to go and bring her back. I sulked and walked to this river from where she would take the boat to go to her parents' home. Her parents lived on the other bank of the river. And here I met Sensei, sitting on the shore of the river." Bodhi paused and looked at Sensei.

"Then?" Amoor couldn't control his inquisitiveness.

"Hoy Sahibji, my good karma! My little master Sensei asked me why I looked so perplexed and agitated. I told him what had happened. Everyone in the village has a deep respect for Sensei. Right there and then, Sensei got up and in one mighty swoop threw me into the river."

"What?" Amoor was shocked. He looked at Sensei with disbelief.

"Wait to hear the rest. I was taken aback. I knew a lit bit of swimming, and after some frenzied movements, I managed to stay afloat. Sensei put out his hand and pulled me back to the shore. Out of respect for Sensei, I didn't know what to say to him. Before I could utter a word, he smiled at me and said, "Bodhi, I am sorry that I did this to you, but you did manage to swim rather than drown! I wouldn't have let you drown anyway, but you did manage to find your balance. Don't let the unexpected drown you at any time. Always help yourself before asking anyone for help!"

With folded hands, Bodhi said, "Sahibji, if Sensei weren't here that day, I would not have learned my lesson. He explained to me that Koko just doesn't need your physical presence. She needs love also. That I should value her above everything else. Master Sensei taught me that the basis of any relationship is the freedom of allowing the other person to be who they are. He explained to me how much difference it would make in my married life if I took some time every day to connect with the person who means the most to me."

Bodhi seemed to be flowing nonstop with his experience. Two big tears hung from Bodhi's eyes.

"Are you alright, Bodhi?" Amoor asked with some concern.

"Oh … Ji … Sahibji, I'm fine. Thank you! So much to share … I wish everyone would understand the importance of relationships. That day, after taking leave of Sensei, I took the boat and rowed it as fast as I could and went to Koko's house. To my utter surprise, Koko ran towards me, crying. We both hugged each other as if we had just fallen in love. I wiped her face and holding her hand, we sat in this boat. There she sat sobbing like a little girl," pointed Bodhi to a corner of the boat. Lost in that moment, Bodhi kept silent.

Amoor didn't want him to stop and quickly said, "What happened after that, Bodhi?"

"Sahibji, after a little while, I asked her what had made her change her mind, and the reply stunned me. She told me that Sensei had visited her that day and talked to her."

"Sensei, what did you say to her?" asked Amoor, eagerly wanting to know the solution given by Sensei.

"Let Bodhi tell you the rest as well, Amoor."

"Ji, Sahibji. Master Sensei explained to her that excessive complaints make a tired person even more irritable after a hard day's work. A home should be a place of relaxation where one can leave all the cares of the world behind. Small issues of life can be discussed at an appropriate time when the partners are at ease, relaxed. Otherwise, those small issues become big ones. Love and peace at home should be our utmost priority. The universe has blessed women with the amazing strength of the earth, which absorbs, nourishes, gives, accepts, and prospers each life that it touches. That's it, Sahibji ... Koko realized her mistakes, just as I had realized mine, and cried so much on seeing me."

"But, how did Sensei know that Koko had left you to go to her parents' home?" Amoor wondered aloud.

Bodhi looked at Sensei with great respect and said, "That I don't know! Master Sensei knows things that you and I don't."

Then he continued, "After Koko came home, both of us had to work on ourselves, change how we had become habituated to live and react in a particular way. Now, no matter how busy I am, I make sure to spend time with Koko, hold her hand, hug her. I now see her as a person in her own right. I value the hard work and love she puts in making the home such a beautiful and comfortable place to come to. Gone are Koko's complaints too. She again knits beautiful shawls and scarfs, hums the songs, waits to see me at the end of the day just as I do, welcomes me with a smile just as I do. Life is beautiful again; we feel like a recently married couple. I realized that it's not the money, it is the people that matter. If we are not happy, if we are not at peace, if we cannot wake up to look forward to life, no matter what we earn or learn – it is all a loss."

The boat had almost reached the shore. Bodhi got up and threw the anchor towards a wooden pole and then jumped in the shallow part of the river to tie the boat. Another journey had come to an end. Amoor and Sensei got up, and Bodhi helped them get off the boat.

"Please wait, Sahibji," said Bodhi.

He went back to the boat and took out another treasure from the box and joined Amoor and Sensei.

"Sahibji," saying this, Bodhi wrapped a beautiful red and gold-colored, hand-knitted scarf around Amoor's shoulders. "Please accept it as a gift from our side. It will remind you of my story to not let go of someone who makes a difference in life. Perhaps you can pass this story to other couples who are lost in the unnecessary dos and don'ts of daily life."

Bodhi bowed with folded hands, and so did Sensei.

Amoor felt very emotional in that moment. He folded his hands in gratitude and with glistening eyes, said, "Thank you, dear Bodhi!"

Bodhi gave a big embrace to Amoor, hopped in the boat, and with a smile on his face, waved them good-bye.

NOWHERE TO GO

What brought me here
in the unknown
land
is perhaps
my hidden
desire
to find
my
lost
self
under the
good looking
sheets of
society
pretending to
fit in
the so-called
good frame
Tired
I escaped
and came here
to the unknown land
and found
my
frame-free
life

The Epiphany

"Amoor, is it getting too much? I see you're going through a lot of emotions," said Sensei with a feeling of concern.

"Nah," Amoor's voice choked with emotional connectivity. "I feel tremendously blessed, Sensei, to meet everyone I met today."

"We are close to your home. If you are not too tired, I would like to take you to a forgotten place."

"Sure, the boat ride and Bodhi's story were an eye-opener. I know now, Sensei, why you had me meet Bodhi. I've realized what I need to do when I meet my Alie! And the coconut water has refreshed me enough to walk. Let's go."

Sensei gave a happy nod and pointed towards a herd of goats and said, "Yes, Amoor, that was certainly refreshing. Now that's where we will go."

Amoor did not understand "where" but followed Sensei. By now, he had learned the magic of going with the flow and was in tune with the more in-depth knowing of the heart.

After half-a-mile of walk through the scattered coconut groves, the scene began to change. The trodden track they were walking on and another rugged pathway merged into one grassy walkway, winding up a mountain. Sensei and Amoor started walking up that path. The goats with the curved horns accompanied them, jumping and climbing, raising their hoofs. The little trinkets around their necks clinked and added lovely sounds to the silence of the now more visible snowcapped mountains.

Soon, the winding path became steep, isolated. The dense pine trees lent a deep green and maroon hue to the mountains. A magical display of flora and fauna colored the rocky slopes. It was quite a spectacular vista of contrasts in nature.

Enroute, on smaller hilltops, big rocks were piled on top of each other in a circular shape with several steps, painted in white, leading up to them. Amoor noticed an old woman kneeling on one of the steps. She was gently rotating a prayer wheel with one hand while holding a rosary in the other. The sound of her evocative prayers vibrated through the tranquility of the surroundings and blended with it.

Amoor did not try to figure out the purpose of the placement of these big rocks, the steps leading up to them, and why they were painted white. He did not even question Sensei about them. He simply appreciated the stunning view.

Here and there, a series of thin streaks of waterfalls lent their music to this magical landscape and quenched the thirst of travelers. Rows and rows of old and new, vibrantly colored flags hung on strings between the trees.

"Sensei, those flags are beautiful! Wondering who put these here," Amoor couldn't help asking.

"These are prayer flags. People in this area believe that as the wind blows, the prayers written on these flags are transported by nature from earth to heaven for the wellbeing of one and all."

"That's very interesting. I would love to send prayers and gratitude too. Where can I buy these flags?"

"Why buy them? Rather, put your personal touch to something that feels close to your heart. It's such fun to make prayer flags yourself. Write your prayers and wishes on them and tie them to a string which you can put in your backyard or someplace high where you can see them fade away as the wind blows and the sun shines."

"Yes … yes, I guess I can become a little creative just like Koko. Or, wait a minute …" he remembered something, "Alie is quite good at it. She will certainly like to do this," chuckled Amoor, walking up the green path, looking around, with a sense of joy.

"Sensei," said Amoor, his mind clear like the blue sky, the clouds had disappeared, "I have so many things to write and send to so many people. Can I write my apologies too? Will they reach as well?"

"You can write whatever you want as long as it is from your heart. The mind calculates heart touches. Heart connections are the strongest. When you do something with all your heart, with all your beingness, with all your feelings, the effect reverberates throughout the skies. Whatever you put out comes back like an echo and in multiples. Your love, your apologies, your feelings, your giving will all return to you."

"Hmm ... I see, that feels good."

"Remember to give out that which you want to receive back. Even the tiniest thought or gesture is not lost in this great universe, never ever!"

"It makes sense! I feel that I've learned so much from you." The petals of Amoor's heart opened and blossomed with this new knowing.

"I'll never let you go, Sensei, never!" Amoor's heart was filled with love and reverence.

Sensei patted Amoor's hand, looked at him intensely, and said, "Amoor, don't be so attached to me. When my part is done, I too will disappear like everything else in this universe. Don't forget, Amoor, that people, as well as events, happen to come in our life for a certain purpose, sometimes to propel us, or to guide us, and sometimes to teach. What has come has to go. Nothing stays forever."

Amoor felt a shiver down his spine. In his heart, he had decided to always have Sensei as his best guide.

The cracks were open
wounds fresh
hurts painful
he looked and looked
at all the scars
complained to god
to world and friends
and those all existed
never fading away
no relief, no medicine
worked at all
for his world
breathed that fall
and then one day
he learned to smile
to love to trust
to forget and forgive
and the antidote
worked so well
all the while
he slept well
he hummed a song
he dreamt a dream
to the happiness he belonged
he lived he lived
a life so full
no scars no pain
just everything beautiful

The Miracle

Amoor's moment of attachment was cut short by the sounds of laughter and giggling as they walked up the path. Initially, the sounds were faint, but as they walked further, the voices grew louder. Amoor became curious as to what was going on.

Soon, they came across a valley. The sight of it transfixed Amoor, and he just stood there with his mouth open. It was something like a mesmerizing scene of a village from a storybook. Above them, a panoply of fluffy white clouds floated slowly, partially covering the pure blue sky.

In the valley was an array of small huts built in a circle, colored in red, yellow, green, blue, orange, purple. The plethora of lush green pine trees stood as guards around them. The trees were encircled with beautiful flower beds in full bloom. There were scores of men there, dressed in colorful, homespun, kurtas. Most of them wore multicolored oval hats. They were busy gardening, building new huts, sawing wood, or just resting under the trees.

Amidst manicured millet, corn, and rice fields was a small emerald-colored lake lending an ethereal sheen to the panoramic scene. Several women were dressed in bright pinks and yellows and greens and blues. They wore beaded turquoise and coral necklaces, hanging down to their navels. Some were busy plucking fresh marigold flowers and collecting them in the cane baskets on their heads. Others were knitting flowers into beautiful garlands as if in preparation for a happy ceremony celebrating life.

The grey smoke arising from a few huts disappeared into the riot of colors spread around them. Dozens and dozens of children could be seen gathered in the center of the village, around the lake. They were laughing and yelling and playing joyfully. No one was interrupting their play.

It looked like a blissful place. There was beauty, there was joy, there was cooperation, there was pure laughter of children. It was a place of abundance. Amoor watched all this, hypnotically, barely breathing. He could not believe that a world like this existed. Everyone seemed carefree.

"What magical place is this, Sensei?" Amoor asked in amazement.

"This?" Sensei paused. He turned towards Amoor and held his hands in his tiny hands.

Amoor shivered again at the feeling of the unexpected. His heart said that he had to be ready for something significant. He held Sensei's hands tightly.

"This is the place where we all ought to be, Amoor. This is the place of joy, of contentment … This is what we are inside us, always like a child — happy, playful, thriving. The colors you see here are the colors of life, of love, of peace, of willingness, of agility, of curiosity that make life beautiful. We are all born with this ease that you feel here today! We are always mirroring ourselves and see the reflection in the outside world. What you saw in your travels today was a kaleidoscope of your life. You, Amoor, you are yourself Kopi, Dara, Bodhi, and this entirety. You just have to find them in yourself. Lost in the cobwebs of the mind, you had wandered away from your true home, which is your real self. But there is always a way to return home, Amoor, that is the magic of life. Today, you have traveled back to yourself. The path was always there; This is where you belong, where I belong, where we all belong – our happy place, our inner home!"

Amoor closed his eyes with tears rolling down. Holding Sensei's hands tightly, he sat down for a long time without moving, without speaking.

"Master Sensei," he finally said. "You have shown me what I can never forget. My heart is filled with love and joy! Oh, Sensei, I feel I'm home ... finally ... I am at home! May the universe bless you!"

Amoor opened his eyes and looked up at the dark clouds. His existence had become like a vast cloud, ready to burst into the rain – the rain of prosperity, of abundance, of gratitude, of appreciation, of a new life. He had never felt like this before. His dam of emotions burst.

"Ah, I am blessed ... I am blessed ... I am touched by the magic wand of the universe ... this joy, this new awareness ... the Miracle has happened ... Yes! Yessss!!! The Miracle has happened!"

Just as he said this, with loud thunder, the rain came down pouring. Thump … thump … thump ... thump … thump … thump … came down the rain, the thunder in the sky mixing with the dum ... dum ... dum ... beats of the drums. Men and women of the village came together and struck cymbals. Trumpets and drumbeats followed. The children danced in the rain. The men danced, the women danced, Sensei danced. Amoor danced and danced!

And then slowly, the rhythms of the music, the joyous cries of the children, and the sound of the dancing footsteps started to fade away. Thump … thump … thump … The rain clouds started to disappear, the giggles of the children became even more distant, the happy faces of men and women began to blur. Then suddenly, with a rumble of loud thunder, a bright light enveloped the whole space. Unable to bear the brightness, Amoor closed his eyes tightly.

"Amoor … Amoor! Can you hear me? Amoor!" This voice was very familiar.

Amoor tried to blink in an effort to open his eyes. In front of him stood his wife Alie, bending over his face, caressing his head.

On the side were his children looking at him intently. Amoor was dazed, unable to understand where he was, what was going on.

"Sensei?" Amoor called, his eyes searching for Sensei, who was nowhere to be seen.

"Hey, Amoor … It's me, Alie!"

"Huh?"

"We rushed here when we heard you were in an accident. Do you remember you were in a car accident?"

"I was?"

"You have been unconscious for the last forty-eight hours. Doctors were not sure if you would survive. We had lost all hope, but I kept praying for you!" Amoor's wife broke down into tears as she touched his face.

"I'm so glad to have you back, Amoor! What would I do without you in my life!" she kissed his forehead, sobbing.

His children had tears streaming down their faces as they hugged their father. Amoor blinked his eyes many times and tried to sit up a little with the help of Alie, still trying to comprehend what had happened.

"Look here, so many people from your office brought you flowers!"

"Ah," Amoor nodded, still in a haze.

"And look at this one! You will be surprised! A small cute boy left this lovely boat-shaped basket with a beautiful red and gold knitted scarf, a flute, a bowl of rice, and look … the basket says – WELCOME HOME! Isn't that interesting! He said that you know him. I forgot to ask his name. Oh, Amoor … your return is a miracle, a true miracle …" Alie wrapped her arms around Amoor, hugging him tightly as if never to let him go.

Amoor responded to her with an intense hug and said, "Yes, my love … I am truly back …" He started to sob. "This was a miracle … a miracle to bring me HOME …"

Tears of happiness rolled down uncontrollably from his eyes as his hands reached for the basket on the table, saying – WELCOME HOME!

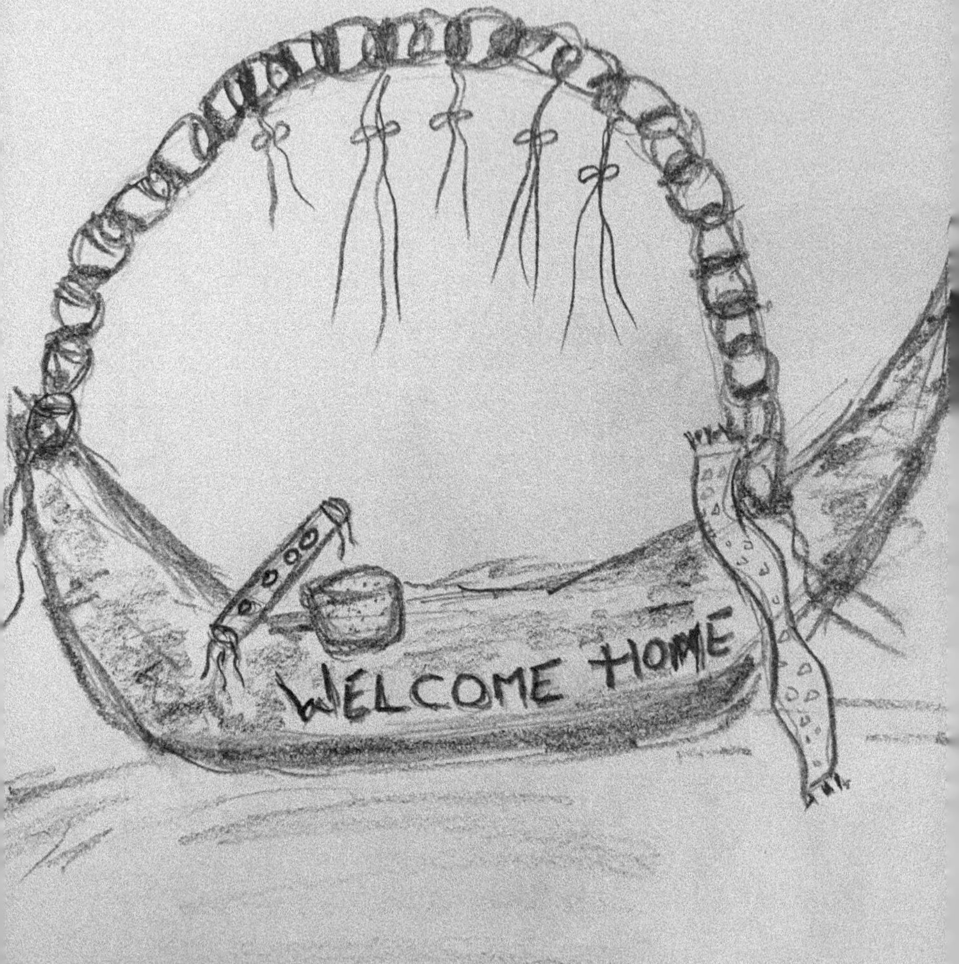
WELCOME HOME

Eyes flutter
like a butterfly
and the sound of
silence
sings a quiet
melody,
somewhere
seven colors
within change and merge
and create halos
of knowing
Mind catches a
flying string
of
lotus heart
blooming
itself with
the petals of
some unknown desires
discovering the
forgotten
self
This is the season –
season of
eternal happiness!

Lightning Source UK Ltd.
Milton Keynes UK
UKHW012021151020
371652UK00001B/226